Why Just Me?

MARTYN GODFREY

Why Just Me?

cover by
Tony Meers

Scholastic Canada Ltd.

Scholastic Canada Ltd.
123 Newkirk Road, Richmond Hill, Ontario Canada L4C 3G5

Scholastic Inc.
555 Broadway, New York, NY 10012, USA

Scholastic Australia Pty Limited
PO Box 579, Gosford, NSW 2250, Australia

Ashton Scholastic Ltd.
Private Bag 94407, Greenmount, Auckland, New Zealand

Scholastic Ltd.
Villiers House, Clarendon Avenue, Leamington Spa,
Warwickshire CV32 5PR, UK

Canadian Cataloguing in Publication Data

Godfrey, Martyn
 Why Just Me?

ISBN 0-590-24919-3

I. Title.

PS8563.08165W4 1996   jC813'.54 C95-933176-X
PZ7.G5434Wh 1996

5 4 3 2 1   Printed in Canada   6 7 8 9/9
                    by Webcom Limited

To Joanne Kellock,
who inspired the changes.

Classic
School
Exercise
Book

Name: **Shannon MacKenzie**

School: **Pine Grove**

Teacher: **Mr. Manning**

Subject: **U.S.S.W.**

The vampire stared into my eyes.

"You're mine now, Shannon MacKenzie," the vampire hissed. *"You'll have to walk with the undead forever."*

How's that for a good start? Mr. Manning, my homeroom, English and Social teacher, says that every piece of writing should have an "effective opening."

Mr. Manning is a new teacher at Pine Grove School and he has a thing about writing. Last Tuesday, on the first day of school, he told us that writing is his hobby. He said he'd love to be a writer.

I can't understand that. Why write when you don't have to?

I *have* to do it. For the last twenty minutes of English class, everyone is supposed to write in a Keytab. Mr. Manning calls it U.S.S.W. or Uninterrupted Sustained Silent Writing.

I call it *a pain!* What makes it really stupid is that Mr. Manning says he doesn't want to read it. As long as he sees us writing, he's happy.

"Why are we doing this if you're not going to mark it?" my friend Rachel asked him.

"For the love of it," he smiled.

I wonder what the other kids are going to write in their journals?

Chuck Hillman, who sits to my left, is writing down all the swear words he knows. So far he's filled half a page.

Jeeny Carter, who sits on my right, told me she's going to write down secret stuff. Knowing Jeeny, that means she's going to write about boys.

Marlene Hodgkin, in front of me, says she's going to write about all the wonderful things that happen to her in seventh grade. I stuck my finger down the back of my throat to show her what I thought of that.

What else can I say?

Today is Monday, September 8.

My name is Shannon Elaine MacKenzie.

I'm almost thirteen.

I'll be a teenager next January 11.

Right now, I'm sitting in the last seat of row three in Room One of Pine Grove Elementary and Junior High School.

I have a brother called Ralph. He's sixteen and is into cars. We get along okay.

I have straight brown hair. Rachel's hair is black and frizzy. Jeeny Carter has blonde hair that's permed. Marlene has tight red curls. Chuck's hair is so short, he looks bald.

I'm super scared of . . .

All right! U.S.S.W. is over. It's home time.

Tuesday, September 9

Another twenty minutes to kill. What do I write about today? Talk about a dumb assignment! Where did I end up yesterday? Oh, yeah . . .

I'm covering this up, just in case Chuck can read it out of the corner of his eye. You can never tell what mutants can do.

I'm not happy about starting junior high because I know my greatest fear can happen at any moment. I'm afraid of growing up. No, that's not quite true. I can't really see myself being grown up. What scares me is THE BIG P. Right — puberty.

Just writing the word makes my hands shaky. This is no little worry. After puberty, I'll be changed forever.

And I don't want to change. Not at all. I'm happy living in this body. I don't want the changes puberty is going to make. But I know it's going to happen soon. It's already started. This summer I noticed little dark hairs under my arms and . . . you know. And my chest started to get itchy and swollen. I don't want to grow . . . you know.

I'd say over half the girls in my seventh grade class are well into puberty. Their bodies have changed — are still changing. They look different and they act different. They sit around in clumps and giggle. The only thing that seems to interest them is hanging out in the Mall or talking about boys who hang out in the Mall.

Apparently this is normal behavior for someone in the middle of puberty. It's because of hormones. Last spring the public health nurse came to the school to speak to the sixth grade girls. She explained that come THE BIG P, our bodies would produce chemicals called hormones. These hormones would change our bodies and also make us change our view of boys. That's sort of like going insane when you think about it.

Jeeny Carter is a perfect example. She started changing in the fifth grade. Now look at her. Boy crazy! I've even seen her holding hands with boys.

I tried to tell my best friend, Rachel Parsons, about my fear, but she didn't really seem to understand what I was saying.

Wednesday, September 10

Oh boy, it's U.S.S.W. again. I'm so thrilled I think I may fall asleep!

Rachel and I have been friends ever since I came to Pine Grove School two years ago. We're really close. She's got a great family — two sisters and her original parents.

Last March, after she told me she'd had her first period, I asked her what it felt like.

"Nothing," she told me. "I was wondering when it would happen. But I don't feel anything."

"Are you scared?"

"Am I scared?" she wondered. "About what?"

"You know," I tried to explain, "about growing up."

5

"What are you talking about, Shannon?"

"Rachel, can I talk to you about something? Something friend to friend?"

"Of course you can. What's wrong?"

"Nothing yet. But I'm worried. I mean, I'm worried about . . . " Then I proceeded to tell her my fear.

She looked as if she was listening to me, but when I'd finished my confession, she started to laugh. "Oh, Shannon, you're terrific. You're the best friend I've ever had!"

"Thanks, but what about what I just told you? What about my fear of growing up?"

"You're serious?"

"Of course, I'm serious. Why would I make it up?"

She scratched her chin. "That's silly."

"Silly? I tell you the number-one scario in my life and you say it's silly?"

"'Course, it is," she said. "Puberty isn't something you can do anything about, is it?"

"But I don't want it to happen."

"You make it sound like you're going to have a heart transplant or something."

I think that was Rachel's way of trying to make me feel better.

It didn't help.

At lunch I asked Mr. Manning how many of his stories were published.

He said, "None. Nobody seems to like them. But I keep trying. I'll make it one day. My ex-wife said I was crazy to keep writing, and

I'm determined to prove her wrong."

It seems an awful waste of time to write stories that nobody wants to buy. Maybe he should concentrate more on being a teacher.

I've noticed that Mr. Manning doesn't get along with the other teachers all that well. They stand in the halls to make sure we walk on the right side of the hall during class change. Mr. Manning sits in the classroom and writes.

I overheard Mr. Wardcourt, the assistant principal, telling him that hall supervision was part of his duties. Mr. Manning told him something about "different priorities."

Thursday, September 11

Oh joy, oh joy, more U.S.S.W.

Chuck Hillman just showed me his list of swear words. Half of them are spelled wrong. Then he showed me how he can stick the tip of his tongue inside his nostrils. A wonderful way to end the day.

And what a miserable day it is. It's cold. I had to wear my heavy jacket to school. I live in the City of Edmonton. It's pretty big, but it's almost near the Arctic Circle.

I've been living here for two years. Before that I lived in Dallas, Texas, where I was born. My father moved to Canada to work in an oil refinery when he and Mom split up.

My mother still lives in Dallas. She left us

after she fell in love with an eye guy. Not a doctor, but one of those people who do eye tests and make glasses. He's goofy-looking and short. My dad is so much better looking, except for his beer belly.

At the time, their divorce hurt and confused me, especially since Mom was willing to leave Ralph and me as well as Dad. Somebody should have explained about hormones at that time.

Come to think of it, it still hurts.

I wish I could see Mom more often than the week-long visit during spring break. And we don't talk on the phone as much as we used to. It's as if the goofy-glasses guy is more important than her kids. At first I wished she would come to her senses and return home. But six months after the divorce, she got married to the goofy-glasses guy.

My dad doesn't have a girlfriend. Maybe he doesn't trust women anymore. His big thrills in life are working overtime and drinking beer in front of The Sports Network.

I've been working up the courage to tell Dad about my fear, but I'm not sure he'd be able to handle it. He's uncomfortable talking about personal things. Last year, when the notes went home telling the parents that the public health nurse was going to talk to us, he was thinking of keeping me home that day.

"Stuff like that shouldn't be taught at school," he reasoned as he thumped his hand on the kitchen table. "Stuff like that should be taught in the home."

"So, you going to tell her about it, Dad?" Ralph asked him.

My father thought for a moment and changed his mind. "Maybe it *is* better to have a nurse tell you stuff like that."

Friday, September 12

We had a dental hygienist visit the class today. She came and told us about Mr. Plaque, like we were still in kindergarten. Then she passed out little pieces of dental floss and the whole class had to practice slipping string between their teeth. Gross!

Chuck Hillman was pulling out all sorts of brown stuff and showing it to me. Gag me with a spoon!

I couldn't take it. I had to tell Mr. Manning.

This is what Mr. Manning said: "Chuck, act normal."

That *is* normal for Chuck. In the fifth grade Chuck had a booger collection. He picked his nose and stuck the stuff under his desk. It was Christmas before the teacher discovered the treasure.

And in the sixth grade he made himself pass out in class and nearly scared a substitute teacher to death.

"You want to see me pass out and freak the sub?" he asked the kids who sat around him.

"Not really," I said.

"Sure," Rachel disagreed.

So he held his breath, placed his hands on the edge of his desk and began to push — real hard. His face went a beet color and little veins started popping out on his forehead. I had a vision of his head vanishing in a red mist.

He was pushing so hard his whole body was shaking. Then his eyes rolled up into his head and he went limp. It was like watching a movie in slow motion. He slumped forward and his forehead bounced on his desk.

The sub went strange. She sent Rachel to the office to get Mr. Wardcourt. By the time the assistant principal arrived, Chuck was conscious and smiling and the sub had collapsed in the teacher's chair.

So that is normal behavior for Chuck. Can you imagine what hormones will do for him?

We had volleyball in gym. Jeeny Carter was excused because she said she had cramps. Just another thing to look forward to.

You know, this U.S.S.W. thing isn't *that* bad.

Monday, September 15

I tried to call Mom on Sunday afternoon. I wanted to tell her about school and talk to her about my fear. I'm curious if she felt the same way when she was my age.

I haven't spoken to Mom since July — over six weeks. When we first moved to Edmonton, we used to call each other every week. But that changed to every two weeks, and now it's once a month at the most.

Yesterday, all I got was the machine.

"Hi, there," her recorded voice sang in my ear. "This is Susan speaking. Neither Morton nor I are able to answer the phone right now. But if you leave your name and number when you hear the tone, we'll get back to you as soon as possible."

I waited for the stupid beep and then said, "Hi, Mom. It's Shannon. I just want to talk to you. Call me when you get a chance."

She didn't call back.

It's strange how things have changed. I mean, three years ago Mom was part of the family. She used to laugh with me, talk with me, give me a hard time — the usual parent stuff. Now she's half a continent away, married to a goofy-glasses guy and living a completely different life.

I still love her. I mean, she *is* my mom. But I don't feel close to her anymore. So much has happened that she hasn't been part of — our move to Edmonton, all of fifth and sixth grade, Rachel, Mr. Manning, everything. And the memories seem more like something I saw in a movie rather than real life.

I was talking about it with Ralph last night.

"Yeah," he agreed, "I have the same feeling. You know, when the folks split, I was really shocked. But now it seems okay. I mean, I wish it hadn't happened. But now everything seems normal the way it is."

"I miss her," I told him.

"Me too," Ralph nodded. "But it's the way it is and we have to live with that, don't we?"

I wish I was older, like Ralph. Then this puberty thing would be behind me.

I'm going to change my opinion on U.S.S.W. I'm going to upgrade it from "not bad" to "all right." Writing about what bothers me makes me feel a little better.

Tuesday, September 16

Last night Rachel and I went shopping in the new mall in Millwoods. Rachel thought it was terrific, but I wasn't impressed. You see the same stores wherever you go. Some junior-high boys were hanging outside the arcade and started to whistle and shout rude things at us as we walked by.

"Bunch of jerks," I complained.

"I don't know," Rachel disagreed. "It's kind of a compliment. It means they noticed us."

Today Mr. Rix, our math teacher, was trying to teach us division of fractions. Talk about useless.

Why would anybody want to divide 6 5/7 by 4 8/9?

It seems like most of the stuff we do in school is a waste of time. I think teachers are just making us do work so they can have a job.

For example, I know how to add. I've been adding since second grade. But every year there are six hundred new addition questions in our math books. Why? How many times do you have to practice adding a bunch of numbers?

It's so stupid. My dad must have done thousands of addition questions when he was in school. But every time he wants to add something at home, he uses a calculator.

I tried to call Mom again last night but got the machine again. I wonder what's keeping her and Morton so busy. What kind of name is Morton anyway? Why would parents want to name a baby Morton?

I remember the first time Mom told me about him. She went to get fitted for contact lenses and came back beaming about the eye guy.

"He explained everything to me," she gushed. "He didn't rush me through to get to the next person. And he was so polite. I'm glad I made the decision to get contacts."

Then she started going back for appointments every couple of days. Dad should have been suspicious. I mean, how many appointments does it take to get a pair of contacts? If I had known then what I know now about hormones, I would have spotted it.

When Dad finally caught on, it was too late. Morton, the goofy-glasses guy, had swept her off her feet. There were a couple of decent arguments between my folks and then she was gone. In fact, she didn't even bother to explain it to me.

"It's for the best, Shannon," she said. "For all of us."

And with that, she moved out.

How can you miss somebody and be angry at them at the same time?

Wednesday, September 17

Chuck Hillman got a raisin caught up his nose at lunch. When no one was watching, he pushed it up his left nostril. Then he was planning to come up to Rachel and me, hold his right nostril, and blow the raisin onto the lunch table. But when he walked over and blew his nose, nothing happened. The raisin was stuck.

His eyes started to water and he had to tell Mr. Wardcourt, who was on lunchroom supervision.

Mr. Wardcourt said, "Act normal, Chuck."

Like I said.

At first the assistant principal didn't believe Chuck was telling the truth. "I am not amused by your humor," he said. "Seventh grade boys do not get raisins stuck in their nose."

"It hurts." Chuck moaned.

"How would you get a raisin caught in your nose?" Mr. Wardcourt asked.

"I was going to gross out the girls. It was a

joke." Then Chuck started to whimper.

Mr. Wardcourt still wasn't convinced. "There is nothing funny about inserting a raisin into your nose. I refuse to believe a seventh grade student would do such an obnoxious stunt."

Then Chuck began to cry. Mr. Wardcourt had to drive him to the Emergency, where they pulled out the raisin with a pair of tweezers.

The really disgusting part is that Chuck asked the doctor if he could keep the raisin. He brought it back to school in a little plastic pill bottle and started showing it around the classroom. After a few screams, Mr. Manning took it away. "I think we're a little too old for show and tell," he said.

Jeeny Carter says Chuck keeps calling her to say that he likes her.

Rachel suggested that maybe Jeeny and Chuck should get together to share a box of raisins.

Jeeny pretended to be angry. "Children. You're still children!" Then she smiled at us. Despite the fact that she's suffering from puberty, Jeeny's okay.

A child. That's a word I can't use for much longer. Already I can't order from the children's menu in restaurants. Not that I'd want to, of course — the sizes are so small. And in January I'm going to have to start paying youth prices at the movies. Even the novels we're studying in English are labelled *Sun-*

Why does all this stuff upset me? Nobody else seems to be bothered by it. Why just me?

Thursday, September 18

Rachel Parsons came over to my house last night. We were supposed to do our homework together, but we spent most of our time laughing. I don't know what it was, but we were just in a silly mood. I haven't laughed like that for months.

I wonder what it is that makes people laugh? Mr. Manning said human beings are the only creatures in the whole world that laugh.

Rachel thinks people laugh to move food through their intestines. She says it makes them more regular. "That's why Mr. Wardcourt is so full of it," she explained.

We laughed at that.

And at Chuck. And at Jeeny. And Marlene. And each other.

"I haven't seen you so happy in a long time," Rachel told me. "You've been so serious lately. You've been really moody."

"I've got stuff on my mind," I said.

"Like what?"

I was about to tell her about my fear again, but figured that I'd only end up being told how silly I was. So I told her about my mom and how I felt like I was growing apart from her.

This time Rachel really listened to me. "It must be tough, Shannon," she sympathized. "I don't know how I'd take it if that happened to my folks."

"Do you ever wish you could turn back the clock?" I asked her.

"What do you mean?" Rachel asked.

"Go back into the past. Be in kindergarten again. Everything was so simple then. Get up. Go to school. Play. Eat. Sleep. Wouldn't you like everything to be like that again?"

"No way," she disagreed. "That was boring."

After she'd left, I tried calling Mom again. This time I didn't get a machine; I got the goofy-glasses guy.

"Hello," he said.

"This is Shannon," I grumbled. "Is my mother there?" Every time I have to talk to Morton, I make sure he knows I don't enjoy it.

"Not here," he answered curtly. Morton does his best to let me know I'm not his favorite person either.

When she comes home, tell her to call me." I deliberately omitted the "please."

"She's going to be late," he said. "She's at her jujitsu class."

"Jujitsu?" I said with surprise. Since when did Mom have anything to do with the martial arts? I couldn't picture her karate-chopping anybody.

"She got interested last month," Morton

explained. "She's doing lots of new things now." He made sure he said *now* long and heavy. It was like he figured he'd rescued Mom from slavery or something.

"Tell her to call me tomorrow then," I said as I hung up the phone.

Friday, September 19

At lunch today Rachel, Jeeny and I went to the first choir practice. Our music teacher is Mr. Gowing. He's okay, but he gets really snarky when you don't stand right or you make a mistake. He takes it as a personal insult if somebody sings off-key. But he's a great music teacher. He really knows his stuff. When we pound out a good song, it makes me feel great.

Jeeny was the first to feel Mr. Gowing's wrath today.

"Ms Carter," he growled, "why do the words you're singing sound like a foreign language?"

"I don't know." Jeeny shrugged. "I'm singing what's on the sheet."

Mr. Gowing exhaled long and loud. "Do you think it may have something to do with the enormous wad of gum you are unsuccessfully trying to chew?"

"I don't know."

"Spit it out!" Mr. Gowing hollered. "And never, ever chew gum in choir. Do you hear that, everyone? Gum and choir are like oil and water. They do not mix."

After Jeeny dropped her gum in the garbage and returned to her place, she leaned over to me and said, "It was only three pieces. It wasn't a wad."

There's a boy in choir who is new to Pine Grove. He's in the other seventh grade class. I don't even know his name, but he seems half-decent. He does have a smile and his hair is wavy over his ears.

Jeeny says he's really cute and that she's going to get him before I do.

"I saw the way he was looking at you, Shannon." She grinned. "He likes you a lot."

"Don't be stupid, Jeeny."

"I know that misty-eyed look." She winked. "But it won't do you any good because he's too cute for you. I want him."

"As if I'm interested," I told her.

He wasn't *really* looking at me. Jeeny's just saying that.

At lunchtime today I went to check the lost and found for my gym strip. Mr. Wardcourt was giving somebody royal heck in his office. The door was closed, but he was yelling so loud that I didn't have any problem hearing his words. He was yelling about "unacceptable behavior" and how he wasn't "going to tolerate such rudeness and lack of discipline."

I figured the kid would be so scared he'd be walking on hands and knees. Was I ever surprised when the door opened and Mr. Manning came out. When he saw me searching through the lost-and-found stuff, he smiled and said, "Beam me up, Scotty."

What's that mean? I know it's from that old *Star Trek* show, but why did Mr. Manning say it? He's so weird.

Monday, September 22

I went to the library on Saturday to get some books on THE BIG P. I figure if I know everything there is to know about it, then maybe I won't be so worried.

I was going to clean out the whole shelf in the health stacks, but then I remembered I'd have to check them out. What would the librarian think of me when I put a bunch of books on puberty on the counter? She'd wonder if I was some kind of prevert . . . pervert . . . whatever. She'd think it was a little odd anyway.

So I just picked out one book, *From Girl to Woman*, by Dr. Joyce Conners. Then I got a couple of *Goosebumps* and a *Garfield Treasury*. I was still a little worried about what the librarian would think, but she just ran the light pen over the codes without even checking the titles.

Dr. Joyce Conners must be related to Mary Poppins. This is the first paragraph: "The journey from girl to woman is one of life's most exciting and wonderful adventures. Your body will blossom and bloom in a miracle of change." Who talks that way?

I know what she's really doing. I can tell this is propaganda. That's a word Mr. Manning taught us in English. Propaganda means you only present one point of view. Your lie seems like the truth. If puberty was so wonderful, Dr. Conners wouldn't have to sell it so hard.

But the rest of the book doesn't look so bad. I've finished two chapters already. The first was really neat in a way. It listed the changes people go through from the time they're born until puberty. I learned some neat stuff:

- the weight of your brain doubles in the first year. By twelve months, it weighs half of what it does when you grow up. (Too bad Chuck's stopped growing at age one — ha, ha.)
- an average two-year-old knows 272 words.
- at three years old, you're half as tall as you're ever going to be.
- two out of every ten boys and one out of every ten girls still wet their bed at age five. (Just goes to show the better sex, eh what?)

Marlene Hodgkin just turned around and asked me what I was writing about. I told her, "peeing the bed." She pretended to be shocked. Marlene is such a bozo. She's so out of it. Then again, maybe it would be okay to be a bozo. You'd be too much of a nerd to worry about stuff like puberty.

Dr. Conners writes: "It is natural for a young girl to be anxious about the approach of first menstruation and puberty. But, by realizing that it is a perfectly normal transition and by being prepared and knowledgeable about the changes, the worry will undoubtedly turn to excitement. What can be more thrilling than 'growing up'?"

Okay. I'm knowledgeable. I'll even accept it as "perfectly normal." But I refuse to be excited.

Tuesday, September 23

Mr. Wardcourt came into homeroom and gave us his first lecture of the year. If the seventh grade is like the other grades, we can look forward to one a month.

He walked into class looking awfully serious and asked Mr. Manning if he could speak to us "on a very important matter."

"Sure," Mr. Manning agreed.

So the assistant principal started to lecture us on the value of toilets.

Honest. Toilets!

Yesterday Shawn Nelson, who sits in front of Rachel, stuffed paper towels down the toilets in the boys' room. Then he flushed them and flooded the floor.

You'd think that Mr. Wardcourt's lecture would be about vandalism. No way. It was about how wonderful toilets were. How they controlled the spread of disease. How the school would be a different place if it had no toilets.

Rachel kept looking at me and scrunching her eyebrows.

Mr. Wardcourt told Mr. Manning it would be a fine English exercise to have the class write an essay on how toilets affect our lives.

Mr. Manning scrunched his eyebrows.

Jeeny Carter says the boys' rooms smell different from ours. How would she know?

I tried to call Mom again last night. This time I didn't get the thrill of speaking to Morton or listening to her recorded voice. All I got was ringing. I wonder why she hasn't called me back? Maybe she's too busy being interested in "new things."

That boy from choir smiles at me every time he passes me in the hall. Jeeny keeps making eyes at him, but he doesn't seem to notice. Even Rachel said he's cute. I think that she really likes him.

"You know, Shannon, I wouldn't mind dancing to a slow song with him," she told me.

That's hormones talking.

Wednesday, September 24

Rachel and I have three days in lunchtime DT. We got caught in the boys' room.

Last night we stayed behind to help Ms

Jenkins, the art teacher, put up some artwork.

As we were getting our jackets from our lockers, I told Rachel what Jeeny had said about the boys' rooms smelling different.

"How would she know?" Rachel wondered.

"That's exactly what I thought," I said.

Rachel looked down the hall and pointed to the door of the boys' room. "You ever been in there, Shannon?"

"Of course not!"

"You ever been curious?" she asked.

"Well . . ."

"Truth."

"Not really curious," I tried to explain.

"Well, I am," she told me. "You want to go in and look? There's nobody around anymore."

I shook my head.

"Come on, Shannon," she coaxed. "I can tell you want to go look."

I glanced up and down the hall. "Okay, but just for a few seconds."

As soon as we opened the door, we started to laugh.

Five urinals in a row.

"They took like funny sinks," Rachel chuckled. She stood against one of them and pretended she was a boy.

That started us laughing so hard that the few seconds turned into a couple of minutes. Mr. Owens, the janitor, came in to see what all the noise was about.

When we were called to Mr. Wardcourt's

office this morning, the assistant principal told us how we'd broken an important rule. "Rules are for the benefit of everybody. If one person breaks one rule, then everybody suffers. Do you understand that?"

"Not really, sir," Rachel said. "I mean, Shannon and I would never have dreamed of going in there if any boys were in the school. But there was nobody else around. Mr. Owens goes into the girls' room when there's nobody around."

Mr. Wardcourt went red and said if she didn't watch it, she'd grow up to be unemployed.

Neither of us understands that.

One thing for sure, Jeeny didn't know what she was talking about. The boys' smells the same as the girls'.

Thursday, September 25

More stuff from Dr. Conners:

— the brain of a seven-year-old is almost as big as an adult's. That's pretty awesome when you think about it.
— nine-year-olds express open contempt and dislike for the opposite sex. I can remember hating boys, simply despising them. I don't feel that way anymore. Now they're okay. Sort of. Although I can't really see wanting to kiss one.

— you heal four times faster at age ten than at age fifty. Looks like I'm over the hill already. And the bad stuff starts at age ten. One in a hundred girls starts her period at ten. Must have been Jeeny Carter.

— at age eleven, it's one in five, and by age twelve and a half it's one in two. The hair and breast thing is well underway as well. That means I've beaten the odds so far. My luck can't hold out much longer.

I found out the name of the new boy from choir. It's Derek Anderson. I think it really suits him.

When I was walking down the hall this afternoon he smiled at me again. And he said hello — really nice like.

Jeeny is going to have competition for him, though, because Rachel has a plan to get him to notice her.

My mom called me last night. We had a wonderful fifteen-second conversation.

"Hi, honey," Mom began. "Morton has only just told me that you called. He's such a dip sometimes." She giggled at that. "Is something wrong?"

"No," I told her. "I just wanted . . . "

"Oh, good," Mom said. "I did get your message on the machine and I was going to call you back when I had the time. But I've been so busy. When Morton said you'd phoned again, I thought there might be something wrong."

"I just wanted to talk about something."

"We'll have to do that," Mom went on. "But not now. I'm just off to an origami class. Do you know what that is?"

"No."

"I'll tell you later. How's Ralph?"

"Fine."

"And your father?"

"Fine."

"I'll call back when I have time. Bye, honey."

I looked up origami in the dictionary. It's "the art of folding paper into intricate designs." I guess that is so much more important than speaking to your only daughter.

So much for Mom. I'm going to have to talk to Dad. I don't care if stuff like that makes him uncomfortable. I have to talk to him.

Friday, September 26

Rachel is really mad because Jeeny spoiled her plan to get Derek to notice her.

Just before choir practice Rachel took the notes off the rings of her binder. She was going to walk past Derek, drop the binder and spill the papers. Of course, Derek would help her pick them up and Rachel could casually mention that there was a new horror movie, *The Slime*, at the Cineplex. Hopefully, Derek would catch the hint and ask her to go.

Everything started out fine. When we walked into the music room, we saw Derek standing by himself. She went over, dropped her binder and the papers flew all over the place.

"Wow, what a mess!" Derek said. But just as he was bending over to help her, Jeeny butted in. "Oh, Rachel, you are such a klutz."

Then she cooed in her phoniest sweet voice, "Derek, can I talk to you alone for a moment?"

"I suppose so," he mumbled as Jeeny directed him to a corner.

Rachel was so angry! I ended up helping her pick up the papers.

And guess what Jeeny wanted to talk about? She asked Derek if he'd like to go see *The Slime* with her! Just like that. How could she get up the nerve to ask him on a date?

But the bigger surprise is — he's going!

For some reason this bothers me as much as it does Rachel. It's none of my business, but thinking about Derek and Jeeny together upsets me. It doesn't fit somehow. I can picture Jeeny holding onto his arm and pretending to be scared.

But, to tell the truth, I think it would have bothered me if he'd gone with Rachel. As soon as she told me her plan, I got a funny feeling. I didn't like it. I mean, it's me he smiles at.

Am I saying that I like him? This is weird. Perhaps I'm leaking hormones.

Rachel's cooled down. Although she stayed pretty angry all weekend, what Jeeny said this morning has settled everything down.

As Rachel and I entered the school, we found Jeeny waiting for us.

"Hi, guys," she said.

"What do you want?" Rachel snarled.

"A couple of things." She smiled. "First, I want to say I'm sorry for Friday. I shouldn't have butted in like that."

"Why'd you do it then?" Rachel growled.

"Because he's cute." Jeeny grinned. "And I figured I deserved first chance."

"It was a gungey thing to do," I pointed out.

"Okay," Jeeny agreed. "I promise I won't do it again. Anyway, after Friday night I'm not interested in Derek anymore."

"What happened?" I wanted to know.

"That's the second thing I want to tell you. All evening Derek kept asking questions about another girl. He has the major hots for somebody else."

"Who?" Rachel asked. "Me?"

Jeeny shook her head. "No." Then she pointed at me. "You."

"Me?"

"Shannon?" Rachel asked.

"You were all he wanted to talk about," Jeeny explained. "It's just like I told you before."

"Me?"

"Derek likes Shannon?" Rachel sounded surprised.

"Shannon was all Derek talked about." Jeeny nodded.

"I . . . I . . . this is silly," I protested.

"I'm sorry, Shannon," Rachel apologized.

"You're sorry?" I asked.

"If I'd known he liked you, I never would have done the thing with the binder. You do believe me?"

"This is silly," I repeated.

All day Rachel has been smiling at me. And when we passed Derek in the hall, she elbowed me in the ribs to make sure I noticed his smile.

I'm pleased and puzzled at the same time. Pleased that he's interested in me. Puzzled because I don't know what to do about it.

In chapter two of *From Girl to Woman* it tells how a little pea-sized gland inside your brain turns on and tells your ovaries to wake up.

Dr. Conners says: "From the pituitary gland, chemical messengers called hormones wake up the sleeping ovaries to prepare for the wondrous passage from childhood. The ovaries then start pumping their own hormones which travel to various parts of the body and say change, change, change."

Why didn't my ovaries say, "No way. We like it the way it is"?

Derek is away today. Rachel heard he's got the flu. I hope he's all right.

Mr. Manning read the class one of his stories today. It was about an alien who came from a planet where everyone was a doctor. I thought that was a pretty dumb beginning, but it got even stupider.

The alien doctor could cure everything from the common cold to heart disease to cancer — everything. He also knew how to stop people from growing older. Everyone would live forever. The only trouble was the alien looked like an orange Popsicle.

Really. How does Mr. Manning think of such stuff?

When the alien landed, it approached the first human being it saw — a seventh grade boy riding his BMX bike. He waddled over on his little wooden legs ready to give his great healing gifts. The boy looked at the alien for a moment, picked him up and licked his head off.

No *wonder* nobody buys Mr. Manning's stories!

I think the boy in the story is Chuck Hillman.

Speaking of Chuck: he ate a spider in Social today — one of those big black ones. It was crawling across the floor. Chuck reached down, picked it up and put it in his mouth.

Then he stuck out his tongue so we could see it all chewed up.

Marlene acted as if she was going to throw up and ran out the room.

I thought Mr. Manning would send Chuck to Mr. Wardcourt, but he just smiled and said, "Perhaps you could find a different way to impress your fellow students."

Is this any way for a teacher to behave?

My chest is growing really quickly. I have to wear sweatshirts all the time.

In chapter three Dr. Conners spends a lot of time on chests. "Perhaps the most obvious change is the growth of breasts. Hormones are busily at work changing the straight girlish shape into the figure of a young woman."

I make sure I put my journal in my locker every night. Until last week I was leaving it in my desk in homeroom. How stupid that was! What if Chuck Hillman had read it and found out I'd written down Dr. Conners' stuff?

Wednesday, October 1

Derek is still sick.

A whole month of school has gone by. That's another thing I've noticed about growing older. Time passes so much quicker. My grandma is seventy. We had a big party for her in Dallas last spring. She said she couldn't figure out how seventy years had gone by so quickly. At the time I thought that was pretty dumb. I mean *seventy* years! They didn't even have TV that long ago. That's how old she is.

Now I'm starting to understand what she meant. It seems like just yesterday Mr. Manning was handing out our textbooks. But it was a whole month ago. I've been worrying about THE BIG P for a long time.

It was warm and sunny today. Rachel and I went for a walk through the grove of trees behind the creative playground in the elementary schoolyard.

"Hey, Rachel, these are all spruce trees," I pointed out.

"How do you know?"

"I remember from fifth grade science. They're all spruce. There are no pine trees."

"So what?" she wondered.

"So the school is called Pine Grove Elementary and Junior High," I said. "The only trees here are spruce."

Then it struck me that the school crest has spruce trees on it. Our report cards have pictures of spruce trees on them. Pine Grove School sends out letters with pictures of spruce trees at the top.

After lunch I asked Mr. Wardcourt why the school was called Pine Grove School.

"Because of all the beautiful trees," he said.

"But there are no pine trees at Pine Grove School," I pointed out. "They're spruce trees."

"They're the same thing."

I was about to tell him the difference when

he said, "Look, Shannon, Pine Grove is a good name for a school."

"So is Spruce Grove."

"Go to class," he said. "You think too much."

How can someone think too much?

Teachers' Convention is tomorrow and Friday so we get a long, long weekend. Ralph is going to a car show in Calgary with his friends, and Dad is going to take me to Jasper for a couple of days in the mountains. I plan to talk to him about stuff like that.

Monday, October 6

You know, I actually look forward to U.S.S.W. It's hard to believe I was so against it. Writing down what I'm thinking seems to make the thoughts a little less heavy. I know that sounds hokey, but it's true.

My long weekend was a wipe-out. I tried to have a serious child-to-parent talk with my dad while we were in Jasper.

Taking a walk in the mountains is my father's only activity outside of work and The Sports Network. He says it "helps put things in perspective." He's not a hiker, just a walker. He only does it two or three times a year and only on well-used trails. And he makes sure that we rent a room in a hotel with a bar and cable TV to recover from the exercise.

Anyway, I figured a mountain walk would be a perfect time to gather my courage and discuss THE BIG P and me.

"Dad," I began as we strolled the shore of Maligne Lake. "I have to talk to you about something."

"What?"

"Puberty."

"What?"

"Dad, I need to talk to somebody about some things."

"About puberty? You want to talk to me about . . . Call your mother."

"I tried to, but she was either out or too busy. Besides, I don't feel all that close to her right now. She's so far away and you're here, Dad."

He stopped and regarded me with an awkward, embarrassed expression. "Shannon, you know I don't know about stuff like that, especially girl stuff like that. Why don't you ask that nurse who spoke to you last year?"

"She was only in for an afternoon," I explained.

He brushed his hair back as if he was thinking. "I'll get you a book. There's got to be some books on stuff like that."

"I've got a book," I told him. "A good one. I know all the physical things. I know about the changes and sex and all that."

He shuffled uncomfortably.

"It's my feelings I want to talk about. It's what's in here." I pointed at my forehead. "You see . . . "

He held up his hands to stop me. "I told you,

Shannon, I don't know about stuff like that."

I thought parents were supposed to help at times like this.

Derek is back. I saw him in the hall twice. Once, when I was by my locker, it looked like he was going to stop and talk to me, but he just smiled and walked past.

"He's probably shy," Rachel said. "You've got to go talk to him."

"I'm just as shy," I told her.

Classic
School
Exercise
Book

Name: <u>Shannon M</u>

School: <u>P.G.</u>

Teacher: <u>Mr. Manning</u>

Subject: <u>Journal</u>

The vampire stared into my eyes.

"You're mine now, Shannon MacKenzie," the vampire hissed. *"You'll have to walk with the undead forever."*

"It's better than living here." I smiled into his red eyes. "Maybe you'll talk about stuff like that."

I'm now on my second Keytab. It doesn't seem almost five weeks since I wrote my "effective opening." Like I said, time is going so quickly.

I spent last night reading my first Keytab. A lot *has* happened that I didn't remember. Maybe getting older means you forget stuff faster.

I'm really glad Mr. Manning is making us write the journals. How's that for a change of feelings?

During library period Rachel told me something I might be able to use.

She was reading a magazine article about starving children in Africa. "This is really awful," she said. "I hate hearing about these things. See this picture of this girl. She's one of the lucky ones. She got help before it was too late."

"She still doesn't look all that healthy," I noted.

"Do you know how old she is?"

"Eight?" I guessed.

Rachel shook her head. "She's thirteen," she told me. "It says here that if you're starving you don't grow up. Sometimes it really hits me how lucky we are."

"Right," I agreed.

I read the article after she'd finished. It seems that malnutrition retards puberty. The hormones don't turn on.

I've decided to go on a diet. That should slow down THE BIG P. Maybe the extra time will give me a chance to get used to it.

First snow today. Just some wet stuff in the air. But, heck, it's only October!

At recess Jeeny Carter asked me if I'd ever had a hickey.

Shawn Nelson showed us how to make rockets. You wrap some aluminum foil around three matches, spread the match sticks and light them. The thing takes off.

Every time Shawn did it, he had a giggling fit. He couldn't stop laughing.

Rachel says, since Derek and I are both too shy to speak to each other, she's going to have to think up another "music-binder" plan.

Wednesday, October 8

We had an English test that went almost to the bell. I'm staying behind so that I can write a couple of paragraphs in my journal. I think

I must be addicted to this thing. Imagine doing schoolwork after 3:30.

I'm hungry!

My stomach was making so much noise Chuck Hillman said I was making "inside farts."

I skipped breakfast and only had a bag of bacon-flavored chips for lunch.

I'm not sure how long I can keep up my diet. Yesterday it seemed like a reasonable move, a way to get a little breathing space. Now it doesn't seem like such a good idea anymore.

Chapter four of *From Girl to Woman* is about menstruation. Dr. Conners spends a lot of flowery words talking about "the miracle that happens once a month . . . the growth and shedding of the uterine lining." She then goes on to talk about babies and junk.

While I was reading it, I almost fell for it. I mean, for a moment I got caught up in the words. It wasn't any thing I hadn't heard somewhere else, but Dr. Conners did make it sound special and amazing, something like a miracle. The feeling lasted for a couple of minutes. Then it dawned on me that once I started, I wasn't going to stop for the next forty years.

This isn't fair. The nurse told us what boys go through but it's hardly anything close to the same thing, is it?

I still haven't worked up the nerve to speak

to Derek. He keeps smiling at me in the halls and saying hello. But he hasn't made a move to speak to me either. Maybe he's not shy, maybe he's changed his mind about me and is just being polite.

Thursday, October 9

I have to stay after school again because we didn't get U.S.S.W. time in class.

My diet is going all right, but I feel faint from lack of food. Only some taco chips at lunch. I didn't even buy a Coke!

The big thrill of the day was the theater group that visited Pine Grove and put on a play in the gym. I'm being sarcastic. The only excitement was the fact we missed math and most of English. After seeing the play, though, it would have been better to divide fractions. What a dopey performance.

It was about getting along with other people — how we should be tolerant of "different" people.

It was so obvious. I think they should have brought the first grade classes.

We were so late coming back to homeroom that Mr. Manning didn't even bother with U.S.S.W.

Instead, we had a talk-time session. He began by asking us what we'd like to talk about. Shawn said we should talk about fire. Mr. Manning said, "That's a hot one." Groan!

We ended up talking about Mr. Manning's writing. He told us he'd just finished a story about the problem of radioactive waste. In his story the government decided to make money out of radioactive waste. Anybody in the country could have as much as they wanted. This solved the problem of disposing of the stuff and improved the economy because everybody had to spend it as fast as they could.

I was going to suggest he write something that wasn't completely stupid. But I wasn't that brave. Instead, I asked him why he didn't write stuff for kids.

"That's a good idea, Shannon." He nodded. "I'm going to think about that."

Mom phoned me last night, but I was at the library renewing *From Girl to Woman*. When I phoned back, I got the machine.

Choir tomorrow. Rachel thinks that the quickest way to get Derek and me talking is to introduce us. That's what she's going to do tomorrow. I'm excited and nervous at the same time.

Friday, October 10

Choir was cancelled today because Mr. Gowing was away. I was disappointed because I didn't get a chance to speak to Derek.

Mr. Wardcourt visited our class to give his second lecture of the year. This time it was on how the junior high students should set a good example for the elementary kids. I suppose he thought this was necessary because Shawn and Chuck were grabbing little kids at lunchtime, holding them upside down, and shaking them to see if any money fell out of their pockets. They got a week lunchtime DT.

Mr. Wardcourt stressed that it was "our responsibility to ensure that the younger children received a proper grounding in appropriate behavior."

Then he said that people who don't learn how to behave in junior high grow up to be outcasts and malcontents.

"What's a malcontent?" I whispered to Rachel.

"Some kind of insect, I think," she whispered back.

Marlene turned around and whispered to both of us, "A malcontent is someone like Mr. Manning."

Mr. Wardcourt finished by suggesting to Mr. Manning that "in light of the circumstances, it would be a suitable assignment if the class wrote an essay on 'The Correct Behavior to Ensure the Future of Democracy.'"

As Mr. Wardcourt left the room, Mr. Manning mumbled something. Nobody heard it, but I could read his lips. He said, "Stupid old fart."

Can you believe a teacher would say that!?

Thanksgiving on Monday. It's always struck me as weird the way Canadians celebrate Thanksgiving so early. It should be in November. For the past two years my mother has called me on the American holiday weekend to wish me a Happy Thanksgiving, and each time I've told her that we had our turkey weeks ago. Both times she's laughed and said, "Oh yes, I remember now. Silly me, I'm so busy doing other things these little details slip my mind." It's become a tradition.

I tried calling Mom last night and got the machine again. This really upset my father.

"I don't want to pay for any more long-distance calls to your mother's stupid machine," he grumbled. "From now on just call her when she's home."

Right.

Tuesday, October 14

Thanksgiving was much different than I thought it would be. Two BIG surprises.

The first was: Mrs. Fox, a neighbor from down the street, came over and cooked us a turkey dinner. She's divorced and has a three-year-old boy, Marty. I've seen her and Dad talking a few times, but I never thought there was anything between them. But there must be. I mean, she came to our place and made a family dinner. Dad, Ralph and I really appreciated the meal. I went off my diet because it would be rude to Mrs. Fox not to pig out.

The second surprise was my brother. After

supper Ralph and I sat in the family room while Dad helped Mrs. Fox with the dishes and little Marty tore through the house.

"Isn't it great about Mrs. Fox?" I said. "I never thought she and Dad were hitting it off."

"It's good to see the old man with some spark again," he agreed.

"What do you think Mom's doing today?" I wondered.

"Who knows?" He shrugged. "It's a regular day down there. She's probably at work."

"So much has changed, hasn't it? Do you ever miss Dallas?"

"Sure," he nodded. "But I like it here too. How are you doing?"

"What do you mean?"

"Just that," Ralph said. "How are things with you? I know you've been trying to call Mom a lot. Things okay at school?"

I told him the seventh grade didn't seem all that great to me. I even hinted about the way everyone was changing and how I was a little frightened by it.

"It'll pass," he said as he held my hand and told me how much he loved me. Honest. I wondered how much wine he'd had with supper.

Then he really surprised me. "Look, Shannon, I know this may be sort of embarrassing for you, but I've noticed you've been . . . filling out lately."

I blushed.

"And," he went on, "I know there's nobody for you. I mean, Mom is so far away and Dad is too thick to notice."

"It's stuff like that," I complained.

He smiled. "When I turned twelve he gave me a book called *Facts of Love and Life for Teenagers*. I think it was written in the fifties and talked about private parts. Can you believe that? Anyway, I don't think Dad knows what to do with you, being a girl and . . . "

We didn't get a chance to finish the conversation. We had to stop talking because Marty Fox overloaded his training pants. There was a puddle on the carpet.

Wednesday, October 15

I went shopping with Rachel and her mother after school yesterday. We went to West Edmonton Mall and we all bought bras.

Ralph had phoned Mrs. Parsons and asked her to do this for me. I'm a little surprised and happy about Ralph. I never thought he had this side to him. I figured he didn't notice anything except cars. I feel really close to him.

After we bought the bras, Rachel's mom took us to dinner at Boston Pizza. I've given up my diet. It was a stupid idea.

During supper Mrs. Parsons asked me personal questions like if I'd started my period. After, she bought me some pads and told me how to use them when the time comes. I already know that stuff from the public health nurse last year, but talking to Rachel's mom makes it seem more normal.

Rachel apologized for not listening to me before. "I'm sorry, Shannon," she said. "I'm sorry I called you silly when you told me how you felt."

"Your mom really helped," I told her.

I didn't have the nerve to wear the bra today. I figured it would be so obvious. So I put on some sweats instead. But tomorrow I'll wear it, for sure.

Chuck just asked me what I was writing about. I told him — a story. He's still writing swear words. Now he picks one word and writes it over and over again for the whole U.S.S.W.

Finally . . .

Derek finally came up to me at lunch and broke the ice. He offered me a piece of his Mars bar and then started talking to me as if I was an old friend. For two weeks I've been worried about how tough it was going to be. Maybe he felt the same way. But all that worry was nothing. It seemed such a normal thing to do.

Most of what he said was about hockey. He told me how well his team was doing and so on. I pretended I was interested in how to shoot a slapshot.

"Boys have to be interested in physical sports," Jeeny said when I told her Derek had spoken to me. "It keeps them from thinking about girls. If you know I mean . . . "

Thursday, October 16

Wearing a bra was something I shouldn't have worried about either. I used to think it would be uncomfortable or that it would be so obvious. But no one has noticed and I have to remind myself that I'm wearing it.

You know, I feel a little different about things.

When Jeeny first got a bra at the beginning of fifth grade, she used to wear baggy T-shirts that would slip down her shoulder. Everybody saw her bra strap and I wondered why she wasn't embarrassed by that. Now I think she was proud that she *could* wear one. I think I feel a little proud myself.

These last few days have been great. Things seem so "up" all of a sudden.

I'm enjoying Mr. Manning's classes. He definitely isn't a normal teacher. He jokes around with us and actually seems to like what he's doing. He sits with his feet on his desk and sings old rock songs to himself.

Everyone likes him. Except Marlene.

In a way I feel sorry for Marlene Hodgkin. She's such a brain. That wouldn't be so bad if she wasn't a nerd as well. It must be terrible not to have any friends.

Today we were reading our Social texts out

loud — stuff about the fur trade in Alberta. After fifteen minutes, Mr. Manning put his book down and said, "This isn't that interesting, is it? Let's do something else."

My teacher said that! Then he told us to put the books away and we had another talk-time session. We talked about getting along with parents.

Rachel thinks Mr. Manning is cool. I think she has a crush on him.

Derek waited by my locker last night and walked me home. Rachel thought that was really neat. "True love," she teased.

Jeeny asked me if Derek held my hand. I told her to get real. Actually, the only thing we did was talk about the Edmonton Oilers and how they were doing on their road trip.

Chapter five in Dr. Conners' book is about boys. Not really about them, but about how girls should feel toward them. "It is a natural part of the maturation process to find a new interest in the opposite sex. A boy with a pleasant smile, a cheerful laugh or even a plethora of freckles can suddenly appear very attractive to the changing girl. It is normal to want to talk to them, to share common interests."

I think I've watched two hockey games on TV in my whole life. Is this a common interest?

Mr. Gowing came back to school today. He could hardly talk. He's had larogitis, laranjitus — he lost his voice.

During choir Derek asked me if I'd like to go to West Edmonton Mall with him on Saturday, and I said okay. At least we'll have something to do besides talking about hockey.

"This is your first date," Rachel said.

"At the Mall?" I laughed.

"I guess it isn't that romantic, is it? But you have to start somewhere," she reasoned.

Pine Grove's principal, Mrs. Haines, came in for a classroom visit this morning. We hardly ever see Old Lady Haines. She just sits in her office with the door closed. Shawn thinks that Mrs. Haines goes home and only pretends to be at school.

But we saw her today. She sat at the back during Social and wrote things in a book.

Mr. Manning seemed a little upset to have her there as we read about fur trade routes.

At the end of the class Mr. Manning said, "So, you see, our country was founded by a bunch of losers who liked living with trees. These people hunted for rodent fur so people half a planet away could wear the fur on their heads."

All the time, Mrs. Haines was writing furiously in her book. After lunch Mr. Manning seemed angry.

During gym Jeeny asked me if I was wearing a bra. When I told her I was, she smiled and said, "Congratulations."

My mom phoned last night and we had a *long* conversation. By that I mean it was at least ten minutes. I told her about my new bra and choir and Derek.

Mom told me about her jujitsu class and origami lessons and how well the accounting business was doing.

She finished by saying, "Any time you need to talk to me, honey, just call. I'm so interested in how you're doing. I'm looking forward to seeing you next spring. It seems such a long way away, doesn't it?"

It is a long way. If she really wanted to see me, she'd come up for a weekend or work out something for Christmas.

I guess life with the goofy-glasses guy is just too exciting.

Monday, October 20

At first I got dressed in my blue skirt. Then I figured it would look like I was trying too hard, so I put on my jeans and a sweater. And I thought about wiping off the little bit of eyeshadow and lip gloss, but I kept it on. In short, I was really nervous before Derek called for me on Saturday and we caught the bus to the Mall.

Although I knew it wasn't a real date, I was

still going somewhere with a boy — alone.

I usually love going to West Edmonton Mall. I could spend a whole day on the rides. And another day in the wave pool and the water slides. If I'm only there for a couple of hours, I'll go on the submarine ride or watch the dolphins in the aquarium. The golf course is all right too. There is just so much to do.

So guess what Derek and I did?

We went to the skating rink and watched the Oilers practice. Really! With all that other stuff to do, we ended up watching a hockey practice.

"You want to do something else?" I asked after a while.

Derek gave me a stunned look. "Like what?" he said.

Two hours of watching a hockey practice!

When the Oilers finally packed it in, Derek took me to TacoTime for a burrito. Then he told me we had to go home because he had his own hockey practice before supper.

"Don't you get tired of hockey?" I asked.

He laughed. "'Course not." Then his eyes brightened. "Say, do you want to come and watch me?"

"No, thanks, I've got ballet," I lied. It was the first thing that popped into my mind. I didn't want to hurt his feelings.

"Maybe next time," he suggested.

I nodded.

I don't want to go sit in a cold arena and

watch his hockey practice. Derek *is* cute and he doesn't seem as dopey as the other boys. I mean, compared to Chuck and Shawn . . . But this hockey stuff is too much.

Chuck Hillman just fell out of his desk. He was writing away and simply tipped over.

Mr. Manning came back and saw Chuck's journal. He flipped through the pages and made a little smile. Then he handed the book back to Chuck.

"I didn't think those two words went together," he said as he pointed to one of the pages.

Once again Mr. Manning proved how different he is.

"Try to think of a few words that don't have four letters," was all he said.

Tuesday, October 21

Jeeny Carter is going out with a boy in ninth grade. His name is Hank Johnston and he's two years older than she is — almost fifteen.

Hank Johnston always wears heavy metal T-shirts and dirty black jeans. And he's dyed his hair blonde and wears it long. I see him hanging around the arcade, playing video games and smoking cigarettes. Every other word he says is a swear.

One time Rachel and I watched him punch a Zaxxon game. "What the ***** you lookin' at, you *****," he snarled at us.

"I'd never go out with someone like Hank Johnston," Rachel told me. "Guys like him only want to do one thing with a girl."

"What's that?" I asked.

She sighed. "They want to make out, dumbo. Sometimes you're so out of it, Shannon. They want to kiss and hug."

Hank and Jeeny were leaning against the fence at lunch. Rachel and I walked by to see if we could hear what they were talking about. We heard Hank say, "So, Mr. Rix gives me a 'D' in math because I cheated on one ***** test."

Later Jeeny told us that Hank was telling her how pretty she was.

Jeeny isn't the only one with a new boyfriend. Our neighbor, Irene Fox, has one too. My father. He took her out for dinner last night. Then they came home and watched All-Star Wrestling on the sports channel. They sat all close and cuddly.

It's sort of weird seeing Dad holding hands with Mrs. Fox. The only lady I ever saw him hug was Mom. But it doesn't bother me.

It used to really bug me to watch Morton kiss my mother. It just didn't seem right. But it's good to see Dad and Irene Fox. I'm glad they're together. And I don't think the goofy-glasses guy and Mom would upset me all that much anymore.

Funny how my feelings have changed.

Derek walked me home last night. We

talked about hockey. Rather, he talked about it. I wasn't really listening.

As he was saying goodbye, he told me that he'd like to watch me dance someday. That threw me off for a couple of seconds because I'd forgotten my lie at the Mall.

"I'm not that good," I mumbled.

Wednesday, October 22
Dad and I went over to Mrs. Fox's house for supper last night. I ended up trying to entertain little Marty. At one point he hit me on the head with a wooden hammer. I almost killed him. There is still a big lump.

Dad and Mrs. Fox are getting serious. While they were in the kitchen, I could hear them giggling like a couple of little kids. Hugging is one thing, but when a forty-year-old man giggles, then it has to be the real thing.

The big news today is the weird thing that happened between Rachel and Jeeny. They had a fight in the girls' room this morning. It started out so innocent. While Jeeny was leaning into the mirror and putting on eye shadow, Rachel walked over and stared for a few moments.

"You look like a sleaze bag," Rachel teased.

Jeeny chuckled. "You're just jealous you don't have a boyfriend."

"I'm thankful I don't have *your* boyfriend," Rachel pointed out.

I know that sounds rude, but you could tell

by the tone of her voice that Rachel was just joking.

"Hank is very nice," Jeeny defended.

Rachel turned to me and held out her hand as if she had a microphone. "Let's get a second opinion on that, folks. What do you think of Hank, Shannon?"

Before I said anything, Jeeny flipped out. She slapped Rachel on the face.

Rachel was so surprised she just stood there with an open mouth. Then she touched her cheek and her face flushed. She returned the attack with two fast punches to Jeeny's head.

"Stop it!" I shouted. I tried to break it up by moving between them. My role of referee was rewarded with a fist in my right eye.

There was so much yelling and screaming that Mrs. Hornblower, a fourth grade teacher, came into the girls' room. Jeeny and Rachel continued to swing at each other even with the teacher there.

Mr. Wardcourt gave them a whole week in lunchtime DT.

Rachel has been quiet all afternoon, but Jeeny is still really angry and squints her eyes every time she looks at me.

What a weird thing. I suppose this is just another example of hormones in action.

Mr. Manning was called out of class during English this afternoon. While he was away, Chuck Hillman entertained the class by making belching noises.

I've had this tight feeling in my lower stomach for a couple of days now. Is this going to be it?

Thursday, October 23

Something is up with Mr. Manning. He was grumpy right from the beginning of the day. Then during Social, Mr. Panek, the superintendent of all the schools, came in and sat at the back of the class the same way Mrs. Haines did.

We were talking about how the fur traders built forts and gave the natives whisky in return for beaver skins.

At one point Mr. Manning told us that the City of Lethbridge used to be called Fort Whoop-Up. "You see," he told us, "alcohol has played an important part in the founding of the West."

Chuck Hillman said he drank some beer at his parents New Year's Eve party and it made him act stupid.

Rachel winked at me.

Mr. Manning then started talking about alcohol and drugs. He told us that it wasn't a modern problem, that almost every civilization in history has had a problem with liquor or drugs.

"Why is that?" Kevin Harke asked.

Mr. Manning shrugged. "If I knew the answer to that one, I could sure help a lot of people, couldn't I?"

As we were dismissed for lunch I overheard the superintendent asking Mr. Manning if he often "presented such an unusual view of history to seventh graders."

"What unusual view?" Mr. Manning asked.

Mr. Panek didn't look too happy. In fact, he looked really upset. I think Mr. Manning may be paddling up the creek with half a paddle.

Rachel and Jeeny are ignoring each other today. I guess that's better than slapping each other around.

I finished chapter six of *From Girl to Woman*. It explained what I already suspected — the fight between Jeeny and Rachel had to do with good old puberty.

Dr. Conners says, "The dramatic physical changes during puberty are often accompanied by equally dramatic emotional changes. The maturing girl can find her emotions stretched and volatile. Relationships with parents and peers can become stormy. Her behavior may bewilder family and close friends. In fact, even the adolescent girl may puzzle at the way the world doesn't quite fit properly anymore."

She goes on: "If your friend is having a roller coaster ride with her emotions, the best help may be a sympathetic ear and some positive suggestions."

This is an interesting thought.

Mrs. Getz, the gym teacher, is having the tryout for the school volleyball team tonight. I think I'm pretty good at volleyball, so I'll join the team.

Friday, October 24

I got cut from the junior high volleyball team. At first practice!

There must have been about forty girls who showed up for the team, including Rachel, Jeeny and me. There's a lot of good volleyball players at Pine Grove and I knew Mrs. Getz was going to have a tough time cutting it down to the ten people allowed on the team. But I didn't think she'd start cutting at first practice. And I didn't expect I'd be one of the first to go. I was shattered.

I didn't think I was *that* bad. Mrs. Getz had said I was really good during regular gym class.

"Don't look so disappointed, Shannon," she said after I'd showered and changed. "I'm sure you'll make it next year."

I didn't think I was so rotten," I confessed.

"You're not." She smiled. "As I've told before, you've got a natural talent for the game of volleyball. But you've got a little growing to do before you make the junior high team."

"What do you mean?" I wondered.

"It's just that the girls in the eighth and ninth grade have a little more maturity on you. They're a little stronger and taller. Give yourself another year and you'll be one of my main players."

"I wish I was older," I grumbled.

I really said that. *I wish I was older.*

Look how hormones are affecting me. How can I say that and be worried about it at the same time?

Rachel was cut too, but Jeeny wasn't. Figures.

When Derek called me on the phone last night, I had Ralph tell him that I was out.

"That's not really fair," Ralph lectured. "If you don't want to talk to him, then tell him. Be honest with the guy."

"It's not that I don't want to talk to him," I defended. "It's just that I'm sort of mixed up about him."

"Okay. But a guy likes a girl who doesn't mess him around. Remember that, little sister."

"Yessir," I mocked.

I'm not "messing Derek around." It's just that I wasn't in the mood for a conversation about hockey.

Monday, October 27

Derek was waiting by my locker when I came into the school this morning. "I'm sorry I didn't call you this weekend. We got back late on Sunday," he said.

"No problem," I told him. "Did you go away?"

"Yeah," he said in a puzzled voice. "I had a hockey tournament in Red Deer. I told you that last week."

I didn't remember. He told me a lot of stuff about hockey last week.

"Shannon, are you mad at me or something?"

I shook my head. "Why do you think that?"

"Well, you don't seem all that anxious to talk to me. And when we walk home, it's like you're somewhere else."

"I've got stuff on my mind," I told him. At least that was the truth.

"And you're probably into your ballet," he added.

Why had I said something so stupid?

"I was wondering if you'd like to come to my game on Thursday night?"

Okay, enough was enough. Like Ralph said, I had to be honest. "Look, Derek," I explained, "in all honesty, I don't really like hockey that much. Not enough to sit in a cold arena anyway."

He seemed shocked. "I thought you really enjoyed hockey. You watched the practice at the Mall."

"My limit for the year." I smiled. "Thanks anyway."

"The arena isn't that cold," he said.

"I have to go," I told him. "Rachel's probably waiting for me in homeroom."

"But . . ."

"I'll see you later." I smiled as I walked down the hall.

When I told Rachel what had happened, she seemed upset. "It's just hockey, Shannon. This is Canada, you know."

"But it's his whole life. Shouldn't we have something more in common?"

"He's such a hunk."

"But we don't talk about anything."

"Being a hunk is enough," Rachel said. "Don't give up on him yet."

This boy thing sure is complicated. Maybe I should try to call Mom tonight and talk to her. No, that would be a waste of time. How can I talk to a woman who married a guy named Morton?

Jeeny and Rachel are friends again. Neither of them apologized, but Rachel said she liked Jeeny's new hairstyle this morning. That was enough to get them talking again.

Jeeny's hair is no longer wavy. It's kind of straight and sticks out. I have a suspicion Rachel probably thinks it's awful.

Jeeny says that Hank wanted her to get it cut that way.

Wednesday, October 29

We had a fire drill right at the start of U.S.S.W. yesterday. By the time we'd paraded out, had the fire people check us and got back inside, it was almost home time.

I was going to stay behind to write but Mr. Manning had a meeting with Mrs. Haines and Mr. Panek, and the school rules say you're not allowed to stay after school if you're not supervised.

Dad took Mrs. Fox to dinner and a movie last night, even though there was a basketball game on TV. He got duded up in his suit.

"This is neat, huh?" Ralph said after Dad had left. "It's great to see the old man so happy. I think that this is getting *très* serious."

I told him how I'd heard them giggling the other day. "You think they'll want to get married?" I asked.

Ralph shrugged. "It's probably a little too early for that. Would that upset you?"

"No," I told him. "I get along all right with Irene. It's just that . . . "

"It's strange seeing the old man with somebody else," Ralph finished for me.

"That's not it. It's Marty. I don't think I could stand living in the same house with the little kid."

"That would be a change, wouldn't it?" he agreed.

As we microwaved some frozen pizza for dinner, Ralph started telling me about a girl he'd met at Mr. Submarine. She'd made him a seafood sub and "me and Donna hit it off real great. I'm taking her to the Halloween dance at my school on Friday."

"Maybe you and Dad could double date," I teased.

"I wonder where she's been hiding out," Ralph grinned. "Donna's terrific and the thing is, she really likes cars."

That made me think of something. "Ralph, can I ask you a question? What if Donna was interested in something you didn't like? What if she was into hockey in a big way?"

"I like hockey," he said.

"But suppose you didn't. Suppose it was a major thing in her life and nothing in yours. Would you still go out with her?"

He shrugged. "I doubt it. I mean, you've got to have something in common. Why do you ask?"

"No reason. I was just thinking."

"Speaking of dates, how are you doing with that guy who keeps phoning?" Ralph asked.

"I'm not sure," I said. "I'm not sure."

Thursday, October 30

Rachel and I spent last evening in the wave pool in the Millwoods Rec Center. It was the first time we'd gone since August.

Rachel and I are big Rec Center fans in the summer. Most of the time we go swimming, but sometimes we go public skating on one of the two rinks. We've even tried playing racketball a couple of times, but we're both too useless to enjoy it.

Rachel wore her new bathing suit and made a big deal of parading around the pool, especially in front of one of the lifeguards.

"Rachel, that's the fourth time you've walked past him," I told her.

"I know." She grinned. "He's cute, isn't he? I was just taking a closer look."

"But he's so old," I pointed out. "I bet he's at least eighteen."

"So what? I can appreciate older men." She laughed. "Don't look so stunned, Shannon. What do you think I'm going to do, ask him out? Jeeny told me to check out the new lifeguard and I was just doing my duty."

"He was looking at you when you walked by."

"No kidding?"

"Yeah," I said. "Each time you walked by he was looking at your rear end."

"He was?!" She struck a pose like she was on a beauty contest. "Some of us have it, I guess."

"Doesn't that bother you?" I asked.

"Does it bother you when Derek looks at you like that?"

"He doesn't do that."

"Shannon, I've seen him. He's crazy about you. You still like him, don't you?"

"Sure," I said. "It's just that . . . "

I didn't know what to tell her. I don't even know how to write it down for myself.

We had to leave the pool early because a toddler threw up. It was all over the shallow end. Rachel's cute lifeguard was trying to clean it out with a screen on the end of a broom handle.

"That's disgusting," I complained.

"Happens every so often, especially in the toddler pool," he said. "But don't worry about it. It doesn't do anything to the water. The chlorine kills all the bacteria."

Maybe he was right, but I'm the type of swimmer who is always swallowing water. Just the thought of it was enough to gross me out.

As we were leaving, we ran into Derek and his mom coming out of the arena.

"We won 6-3," Derek told us.

"Blew the other team off the ice." His mom grinned. "Derek blasted the puck right through the goalie's pads."

Like mother, like son, I thought.

Halloween

I wasn't going to go out this year. I mean, I am getting too old for trick or treating and my dad always hates it when the big kids come around. But Rachel has talked me into it.

"It could be our last chance," she said. "Next year we won't be able to do it. Grab the gusto, huh?"

Why not?

As usual, we had a Halloween parade this afternoon. Everyone dressed up and we made a tour of the other classrooms in the school. I got a charge out of the little kids. They seemed to be more stunned than excited. I guess it's sort of scary to see us big guys dressed up in weird outfits.

Mr. Manning dressed in this old-looking costume with lace cuffs and a bib. He looked like an actor on a PBS show.

"Who are you supposed to be?" Rachel asked. "Are you an old king?"

"Close." He smiled. "I'm the king of writing, William Shakespeare."

"Who's William Shakespeare?" Chuck asked.

Chuck's costume consisted of a lot of crumpled-up tissue paper taped to his body. It was all over his clothes. He even had it stuck in his hair. Everybody tried to guess what he was. I thought he was supposed to be a snowflake. Jeeny thought he was a cloud. Kevin Harke thought Chuck was a piece of cauliflower.

"You're all wrong," Chuck laughed. "I'm a used Kleenex."

Shawn Nelson was a fireman. Or fireperson. Or whatever you call them.

Jeeny dressed in Hank's clothes. They suited her new haircut.

Marlene was a ballerina. Barf me out.

Derek was a hockey player. Why doesn't that surprise me?

Mr. Wardcourt was himself.

Mrs. Haines was nowhere to be seen.

And me. Well, I was and still am, as I sit here, Pandora. I'm dressed as a Greek lady and I have this big box that I painted brown.

Not many of the kids know who I'm supposed to be. We read a story about Pandora in our fifth grade readers. She was the lady who opened a box of demons that brought confusion and chaos to the world.

I figure I can identify with that.

Chuck asked me if I was supposed to be a stripper.

Monday, November 3

I had a great Halloween. This year we got a lot of little chocolate bars and not many suckers and junk. And no homemade stuff. I guess people are finally catching on that kids don't eat the homemade things.

When I was a little kid, I remember Mom and Dad checking out my candy before I was allowed to eat anything.

"People put pins in things," Mom explained to me. Why would anybody want to do that? Just thinking about somebody like that scares me.

While Rachel and I were collecting our sugared loot, we ran into Shawn Nelson on 79th Street. He wasn't trick or treating. But he was carrying five paper lunch bags.

"Guess what's in here?" he asked.

"Candy that you stole from little kids," Rachel said.

"No. It's dog dirt."

"Tell us another." I laughed.

So he showed us. Sure enough, every bag was full of dog poop. We just stared at him.

"Took me a long time to find it all," he told us.

"As long as you're having fun," Rachel said.

Shawn smiled. "Oh yeah, you can have a great time with this. Do you know that most people wear slippers in their houses?"

"So what?" Rachel said.

"So watch this."

Shawn checked out the houses, then dashed up to someone's front door. He placed the bag on the ground, pulled out a match and lit it on fire. He rang the doorbell, yelled "trick or treat" and ran back to us.

This big guy opened the door, looked at the flaming bag and started to stomp it out.

With his slippers!

Needless to say, there was a royal mess.

Shawn ran away carrying the other four bags and laughing like Dr. Frankenstein does in the old movie.

Rachel and I ran away too, just in case the man thought we did it.

To tell the truth, even though it was stupid of Shawn, we laughed too. But not like Dr. Frankenstein.

Derek called me on Saturday to ask if I wanted to go to a movie. I told him that I'd already made plans to go to Rachel's. It was true, but Derek sounded as if he thought I was making an excuse.

Tuesday, November 4

I'm staying after school to write a few words. We didn't do U.S.S.W. today because Mr. Manning read us one of his stories. This time it sort of made sense.

It was about a girl who could read other people's thoughts.

This poor girl got tired of all the stupid stuff people were thinking. She had to put up with thoughts like:

"Rodent fur makes good hats."

"People who break rules grow up to be unemployed."

"Mr. Plaque is the enemy of teeth."

The girl became so confused that she had to go live in the middle of Antarctica among a bunch of penguins.

All she heard in the penguins' minds was:

"I'm hungry for a fish."

"Let's go for a swim."

"Watch out for the killer whale!"

Things were so much simpler.

Mr. Manning sure is a *weird* guy.

I thought about what is going on in Derek's brain:

"Give me the puck."

"Pass me the puck."

"Where's the puck?"

I can see Derek leaning on the bike racks waiting for me. He sure looks good in his new jean jacket. It looks like he's reading a hockey magazine. No doubt, I'll get to hear the exciting "behind-the-scenes" story of someone's jock strap.

I'm being nasty.

Jeeny got cut from the volleyball team yesterday. "I don't really care," she said. "Playing volleyball is for gorfs anyway."

I have no idea what a gorf is. Maybe it's a Hank Johnston word.

I've got to take *From Girl to Woman* back to the library tonight. Dr. Conners helped me out, I think.

Another Keytab finished.

Classic
School
Exercise
Book

Name: __S. E. M.__

School: __Spruce Grove J.H.__

Teacher: __Mr. M.__

Subject: __Journal #3__

The vampire stared into my eyes.

"You're mine now, Shannon MacKenzie," the vampire hissed. "You'll have to walk with the undead forever."

"It's better than living here." I smiled into his red eyes. "Maybe you'll talk about stuff like that."

"You mean you want to be a vampire?"

"You get to wear nice clothes," I pointed out.

A new Keytab and a new outlook. I've decided to meet this puberty thing head on. All this time I've been moaning about it.

I looked at myself in the bathroom mirror after I got out of the shower this morning. My body has definitely changed in the last few months. It's scary. I started to wish that I . . .

Then it hit me. I was doing it again! I was wishing things wouldn't change, that they'd stay the way they'd always been. But for the last few weeks I've understood that things *have* changed. Even when I was hoping they wouldn't, they were.

Well, I'm going to help myself by helping others. Dr. Conners said we should lend a sympathetic ear and give positive advice to our friends who are suffering from puberty. If I can straighten my friends out, I figure it'll help me come to grips with my feelings.

I'm going to take the cow by the ears, as my grandma says.

Jeeny just smiled at me. She looks like King Tut. She has so much eye shadow on, it's a wonder she can blink.

She'll be my first project. I'm going to set Jeeny straight. I'll help *her* sort everything out.

Then I'll work on Derek. And maybe Chuck.

I'll even try to help Mr. Manning get along better with Mrs. Haines and Mr. Panek. I'll tell him how real teachers act, so that he won't get into trouble anymore.

Yeah, I'll help everybody. And by helping everybody, I'll help myself. Why didn't I think of this before?

'Course, maybe Chuck is beyond help. He's sticking his finger in his ear and licking the ear wax.

Thursday, November 6

I asked Jeeny to stay after class yesterday, but she was too anxious to get outside to meet Hank Johnston.

When I told her that I wanted to talk to her about boys, her eyes lit up and she promised to call me later.

"Come by my place after supper," I said.

It felt funny to have Jeeny in my house. We always talk at school and she's one of my friends, but we never do anything together outside of school. This was the first time she'd been over.

I could smell cigarette smoke on her breath.

"You got a nice place," she said as she sat on the end of my bed. "So what do you want to talk about? Something you don't understand about Derek?"

"I understand all I need about hockey pucks. It's not about Derek, Jeeny. It's about you."

She frowned. "About me?"

"You and Hank," I added.

The frown turned into a slight smile. "I knew all the girls would be curious."

"You're right. We're curious why you're going out with him in the first place. Look, Jeeny, I'm your friend and I have a responsibility to tell you that you're being stupid. I think that I can help you straighten yourself out."

Jeeny narrowed her eyes and it was obvious she had got real mad real fast. She stood up and walked to my door.

"Jeeny," I said, "I'm not giving you a hard time. This is positive criticism. I want to help you. Do you know what everyone thinks about Hank Johnston? Do you know what the kids say about you?"

Jeeny gritted her teeth and pointed a shaking finger at me. "What makes you think . . . " She stopped and drew a sharp breath. "I don't need it from you too!"

She stomped out of my room and out of my house.

"Who was that?" Dad asked me later. "I don't think I've met her before."

"Jeeny Carter," I told him. "You met her when I did the skit in the fifth grade concert. She was my partner."

"You mean that's the cute little girl with the curly hair?"

"The very same."

"She certainly has changed," Dad noted.

"Yeah," I agreed. "There have been a lot of changes going on."

Friday, November 7

I struck out with Derek too. After choir I told him that I thought he was hockey crazy.

"Hockey crazy?" he puzzled. "What do you mean?"

"Just that," I explained. "Hockey is the only thing you think about. It's on your mind all the time. Every time we talk it's about hockey. You should take up some other activities."

"Like what?"

"Anything. Swimming or watching TV. Stuff like that," I suggested.

He looked at me as if I had blown a baffle. "Is this a joke?"

"'Course it isn't," I said seriously. "You have a problem because all you ever think about is hockey. As your friend I'm trying to help you."

"That's not all I think about, Shannon."

"Oh, yeah," I challenged. "So what else are you interested in?"

"Well, I used to be interested in you," he said. "I used to think about how nice you were."

I didn't know what to say.

"Why have you been lying to me?" he asked.

"Huh? Lying?"

"Rachel told me you don't take ballet lessons."

"She did?"

He nodded. "You were lying so I wouldn't bother you, weren't you?"

"It was only one time," I defended. "I don't even know why I said it."

"You know, Shannon, when I play hockey I feel good. What makes you feel good? Hurting other people?"

"No . . . I haven't hurt anybody."

"When I found out you'd been lying to me, it didn't feel all that great. And what you just said to me hasn't thrilled me too much either."

Again, I didn't know what to say.

"I'll see you around," he said softly. Then he walked away.

How come he couldn't see I was only trying to help him?

How come I feel so rotten?

Why didn't I mind my own business?

I had a terrible weekend. All I could think about was Jeeny and Derek and how I'd upset them. It seemed like such a good idea last week. I really thought I could help them. Instead, I was an utter and complete jerk.

"You sure were," Rachel agreed when I confessed what I'd done. "How could you have been so stupid? I'm glad you didn't try to straighten me out. I'd hate to hear what you think about me."

"What am I going to do?" I moaned.

"You have to apologize, of course," Rachel said. "Tell them you were temporarily insane."

I must have been. Hormones are messing me up.

I told Jeeny I was sorry in homeroom this morning. She mumbled a "forget it," but she hasn't made any effort to be friendly.

Derek doesn't even look at me when we pass in the hall. What if he just ignores me when I try to talk to him? He did say he "*used* to be interested in me."

We had our Remembrance Day assembly today since tomorrow is a school holiday. An old guy with a funny hat came in and talked to us about sacrifices. He explained how we wouldn't have all the neat stuff we have now if millions of people hadn't died in past wars.

I'm grateful for what those people did so many years ago, but it's just another thing I don't understand. It seems the countries we were fighting against then are now our good buddies.

Why fight a war in the first place if you're only going to end up liking your enemies?

Wednesday, November 12

I think I'm catching a cold. I mean, I think I've caught a cold. I've got a sore throat that's been getting worse all day. And I feel too warm. Maybe I'll be able to get a day off school for this one.

Dad doesn't let me stay home unless I'm half dead. "If you act sick, you get sick," is his idea of how illnesses work.

I just thought about Grandpa Robert, my dad's father. He died when I was five. But I had the sudden memory of him visiting me while I had the chicken pox.

I can see him putting his hand on my head and saying, "Are you feeling poorly bad, Shannon?"

Isn't it weird I remember that right now? I wonder where the memory has been hiding for so long. It makes me think of all the other stuff I've forgotten.

Poorly bad. What a cute way of saying sick. I wish I'd have known him better.

I didn't do much on the holiday yesterday. Rachel and I went to West Edmonton Mall and hung around for an hour or so. They stopped the rides at eleven o'clock for a minute of silence. It was kind of freaky. The place is usually so noisy.

Anyway, we didn't have much money so we ended up going home to watch the soaps on TV. Every time I see those shows I wonder what the big thrill is about being an adult.

I still haven't spoken to Derek since we had our talk. I think I'll forget the apology. It won't do any good anyway. He did say "used to be interested in me." He's already told me what he thinks about me. I'll just leave everything the way it is.

At least Jeeny seems to have forgiven me for being so rude to her. She told me she's going to a party at Hank's place on Saturday. She says Hank's mother won't be home and only ninth grade kids are going.

Chuck asked her if he could go, and Jeeny started laughing so hard I thought she'd wet herself.

Monday, November 17

I wish I could take back what I said about hoping for a day off. Did I ever get sick!

On Thursday morning my throat was so sore I couldn't even swallow orange juice without crying. I know that sounds wimpy, but it's true. I thought it was game over. I had a fever of 3,000 degrees and my back and legs ached so much I couldn't get comfortable, no matter which way I tried to lie in bed.

Dad called the doctor, who asked if I could come into the office. Fat chance! When Dad said he thought I was too sick to go out, the doctor told him it sounded like the flu and there wasn't all that much she could do about it anyway.

"The doctor says drink juice and stay in bed," Dad told me.

"Arrgh," I groaned at him.

It was Saturday before I felt like getting up. By that time my nose had started to run as if I had a tap in my head. It's so red today that Chuck keeps calling me Rudolph. I tried to breathe all over him.

Mrs. Fox came over Saturday and Sunday and cooked the meals and helped take care of me. We had a woman-to-woman talk about all sorts of things, including THE BIG P.

"Everything you've said sounds perfectly normal to me," she told me.

"You mean, you worried about it too?"

"I was petrified," she confided. "Absolutely petrified. I have this thing about blood. So you can imagine how I felt about my first period."

"It doesn't scare me as much as it did a couple of months ago," I said.

"That's what happened to me," she went on. "The thought of something is worse than the real thing, isn't it?"

I guess.

I enjoyed having Mrs. Fox around. I

wouldn't mind her being around on a more formal basis, if Dad wants to marry her. But I'm still not sure about little Marty. He spent the weekend wandering about the house and searching through the closets and drawers. Once he came down with a fistful of my underwear in his hands. I almost gave him a nose transplant.

Rachel said they started rehearsing Christmas carols in choir Friday. Only another six weeks until Christmas. If I was five years old that would be forever. Not anymore.

Jeeny is away today. Maybe she has the same flu.

Tuesday, November 18

Last night as Rachel and I were walking home Kevin Harke pedalled beside us on his bike and told us the incredible news. We found out why Jeeny Carter hadn't been at school all day.

"Hey, guys, guess what I just heard?" Kevin began. "My brother, Steve, is in the same class as Hank Johnston. You're not going to believe this, but last Saturday Hank had a big party that was busted by the cops."

"No kidding?" Rachel said. "What was going on?"

"It was an open house," Kevin explained. "Hank had invited some of the ninth graders but people from high school showed up. They were making all sorts of noise. When the neighbors complained, the cops came and found a few of them were drinking and nobody was eighteen."

"No gufferooni?" Rachel grinned. "Imagine that, Pine Grove has its own scandal. How come we didn't hear about it before?"

"That's because a couple of Hank's buddies don't go to school and they've been in trouble with the cops before," Kevin explained.

"So?" I asked.

"So everyone who was under sixteen had to go down to juvenile hall for a meeting with a social worker."

"All right!" Rachel slapped her hands together. "That's kind of like going to court, isn't it?"

"Not really," Kevin said. "It's just a meeting with the parents."

"Jeeny," I said.

"Jeeny?" Kevin and Rachel parroted together.

"Jeeny told me she was going to that party," I told them.

"Jeeny Carter got busted?" Rachel gasped. "We know a real juvenile delinquent."

I can just imagine how Jeeny's folks took the news. I can picture my dad's face if it was me.

Whatever had happened with her parents, it sure made a difference in the way Jeeny looks. She came to school today with her hair combed. And no makeup.

She looks like a different person.

Mr. Manning smiled at her when she came into homeroom. "How's it going, Jeeny?" he asked.

"The pits."

"This too shall pass," he said. "You look very nice today."

She actually growled.

A few moments ago Jeeny found me staring at her. She sneered and gave me the finger.

Wednesday, November 19

Last night Jeeny came to my house and wanted to talk to me. I was really surprised to see her standing on my doorstep.

"Can I come in?" Jeeny asked. "I'd like to pick up where we left off in your room."

"I said I was sorry about that," I told her.

"Maybe if we'd talked I wouldn't be so deep in it," she reasoned.

So we went to my room and Jeeny spoke to me in a way nobody ever has before. Even Rachel hasn't opened up the way Jeeny did.

She told me how her mom and dad were always fighting.

"I guess you went through that when your parents divorced, huh?" she asked.

"A little," I told her.

"I don't see why my folks are staying together. You should hear what they say to each other. If Hank ever said anything like that to me, I'd dump him on the spot."

She went on about how she had to babysit her little brothers all the time. And how no one ever listened her. Except Hank.

"Sure, Hank is a bit of a jerk," she explained, "but he doesn't act like a little kid and he doesn't treat me like a little kid."

Then she explained how her mom had told her to "clean up your act or get out of the house." And how the world seemed so crazy and how nothing made sense. How much she'd needed someone to talk to. And how sorry she was for giving me the finger. And then she started to cry.

And for some dumb reason, I started to cry too. What a scene. Jeeny Carter and me holding onto each other and crying.

"Thanks for listening to me," she finished. "You've really helped me out."

It's great how you can help somebody without giving any advice.

I told her my feelings about puberty and growing up and the things that didn't quite fit in my life, like my mom. Jeeny listened to me and nodded and hum-hummed at the right moments.

When I was done, we both started crying all over again.

All day I've been feeling great.

For the last two days, every time Jeeny and I look at each other we break into wide grins. It's so stupid.

"What's with you and Jeeny?" Rachel wonders.

Marlene told Jeeny that her "present appearance is more appealing to our sensibilities." That started Jeeny and me laughing for a good five minutes.

Something is up with Mr. Manning again. Mrs. Haines and Mr. Panek both sat at the back of the room during Social. This time Mr. Manning didn't seem upset. He was talking about the Aztecs from Mexico.

"The Aztecs believed in a legend," he told us. "It was a prophecy that one day an army of powerful gods who were half person, half animal, would come to destroy their cities. Then one day the Spanish, who were searching for gold, arrived on horseback in the land of the Aztecs. The Aztecs, having never seen a person on a horse before, figured these were those gods and it was the end of the world. They closed up shop and got ready to die.

"Well, when the Spanish discovered that the Aztecs had a lot of gold, they were happy to help out. So a grossly outnumbered Spanish force managed to defeat a rich and powerful civilization because the Aztec warriors were afraid of a story. And the legend came true."

Just then Mr. Panek interrupted. "What exactly are you trying to say? I've never heard this material presented this way. What is the point of your lesson to this class?"

Mr. Manning smiled. "I'm not sure. Take your pick: wrong thoughts can really hurt you, the pen is mightier than the sword, a little knowledge is a dangerous thing, whatever."

By the look on his face, it was obvious Mr. Panek wasn't impressed by my teacher's answer. He wrote something in his binder and stomped out of the room. "We'll discuss this later, Mr. Manning," he threatened.

Poor Mr. Manning.

I've been thinking about the Aztecs and the Spanish all day. Do I have any wrong thoughts?

Friday, November 21

I went into homeroom at lunch to talk to Mr. Manning. He was working at his desk.

"Hi, Shannon," he smiled. "You forget something?"

"No. Are you writing a story?" I asked.

"I sure am. It's a story for young people. I've taken your suggestion. I can't tell you what it's about yet because I haven't quite figured it out myself."

"Maybe you'll read it to us when you're finished?"

"Maybe," he agreed. "Now what can I do for you? Why are you here? If Mr. Wardcourt finds you wandering the halls, no doubt you'll get forty years lunchtime DT."

I laughed. "I wanted to talk to you. I've been thinking about what you said in Social yesterday. About wrong thoughts."

He waved his hand in the air. "Don't take that too seriously. I was just raving on. Between you and me, I really said it to bother Mr. Panek."

"But it's true, isn't it?" I went on. "Sometimes you might have an opinion about something that's wrong."

"There are many times in your life when your opinion is going to be wrong. We make mistakes and change our point of view. With each change we become a little wiser and a better person." He started to chuckle. "I sure do sound like a teacher, don't I? Do you want to talk about something that's bothering you?"

I shook my head. I don't really know what I want to say or write. But the whole idea about "wrong" opinions is interesting.

"Is that it?"

"Mr. Manning, Rachel and I are kind of wondering . . . "

"Wondering what?" he asked.

"Well . . . are you in trouble with the superintendent?"

He laughed so loud it actually made me

jump. "There's no putting anything past you and Rachel, is there?"

I felt my cheeks flush. "We're not being nosey," I added quickly. "We're just worried about you."

"Shannon," he said, "you tell Rachel I'm exactly where I want to be with the superintendent. Exactly. There's nothing to worry about."

I wonder what that means?

Monday, November 24

Mom called yesterday. And for the first time in three years I felt good after I said goodbye.

"Hello?" I said as I picked up the phone.

"Shannon?" she asked.

Who else would it be? "Hi, Mom."

"I finally managed to get you. I've been calling all day." Her voice revealed she was a little peeved about this fact. "Where have you been?"

"At a friend's house," I told her.

"Did your dad take you visiting on Thanksgiving weekend?" she wanted to know.

"Thanksgiving weekend?" I thought for a moment. Right, last Thursday was American Thanksgiving.

"Canadian Thanksgiving was weeks ago, Mom," I told her. "Remember? They're on different days."

There was a moment of silence and a

chuckle. "Of course. How could I be so silly? I'm so busy it just seems to slip my mind. Next year I'll remember. You must think I'm such a dimbo."

And right at that moment I got very angry with my mother. Suddenly I could think of much better words to describe my feelings for her.

"Well, I feel sort of foolish," she went on. "Morton and I have been watching the NFL on TV and I've just made a big batch of pasta salad for dinner and . . . "

"Pasta salad?!" I interrupted. "You're having pasta salad for Thanksgiving dinner? What happened to turkey and roast potatoes and yams and stuff? Have you given up eating real food, too?"

I could tell she was taken aback by my comment. "It's the thing right now," she defended. "Morton bought me a pasta machine. He's very health conscious, you know. We make our own pasta. It's a much more civilized meal than stuffing yourself with turkey and dressing."

"Morton has always struck me as a gorf," I told her. "And your dinner sounds terrible."

"Shannon!" The edge came back into her voice. "I won't tolerate that. I don't appreciate it."

"You know, Mom, someday when you're not folding paper or kung-fuing or making pasta, give me a call and I'll tell you the things I don't appreciate from you."

"What do you mean by that?" she demanded.

"You want to speak to Ralph?" I asked.

"Shannon, I asked you a question."

"I'll go get him," I said as I put the phone on the table. "Ralph!" I shouted.

Then I broke into a broad grin.

She deserved that. She deserved to know how angry I've been for three years. And I needed to show her.

Tuesday, November 25

After school.

I was going to write more about Mom today, but something else is more important.

IT happened today.

I'd just taken my U.S.S.W. Keytab from my English binder and I knew I'd started. I'm not sure how, but I could tell. I didn't feel wet and there weren't any cramps. It was just a full feeling below my waist.

"This is it, Shannon," I said to myself.

I didn't panic. I checked myself, then asked Mr. Manning if I could be excused. I got the bag from my locker and went into the washroom. It wasn't a surprise to see the blood. I wasn't scared either. I felt two feelings, curiosity and relief.

Now I don't have to be frightened of it anymore. It's happened and I only have to worry about handling it. And, hey, so far I'm doing very well, thank you.

I stared at my underwear for a few moments before taking a pad from the bag and cleaning myself up.

So that's it.

Official puberty.

For some reason, I picture a news anchorman in my head. "And on the National tonight, Shannon MacKenzie of Edmonton has made it official . . . "

I told Rachel at home-time bell.

"Do you want to talk to my mom?" she asked.

"Everything is under control," I said.

Then she started smiling and gave me a hug as the class was leaving.

"Always knew there was something strange about you two," Chuck commented.

"What's up?" Jeeny asked us.

I told her after everyone had left.

"That's terrific," Jeeny said.

Part of me can't believe it. Not about my period. I knew it had to come. In fact, I'd even worried a few times in the last couple of weeks why I *hadn't* started. What I'm having trouble believing is that I'm sitting alone in homeroom writing about it so calmly. Maybe hormones are necessary, maybe they make it seem normal.

"You must have something pretty important to write about," Mr. Manning just said. "It's almost four. Care to share it?"

"It's personal," I told him.

He nodded. "Carry on then."

I don't really have anything else to say.

It just is.

Wednesday, November 26

When I told Dad what had happened in school, he gave me a hug and tousled my hair. "My young lady," he said.

That was sort of a surprise.

He also gave me a $20 bill and told me to go out and buy what I needed. "I don't know much about stuff like that, Shannon. But I'm sure that if you need anything, Irene will be glad to help. She really likes you."

"I know, Dad. I spoke to her before."

That seemed to please him.

Then I called Mom. My day was full of surprises. I didn't get a machine or Morton.

"It's me, Mom," I said. "I just called to tell you a couple of things. First, I'm sorry about what I said on Sunday."

"You really upset me." she said. "I hardly got any sleep on Sunday night thinking about it."

My first reaction was to say, "What about last night?" but I thought better of it.

"Mom, I haven't been feeling all that close to you lately and I'm probably going to say more stuff that's going to upset both of us in the future, but I don't want you to fade out of my life."

"I'd never do that," she said.

"It could happen. And I don't want it to. I think I still need to share things with you."

"Of course, honey. I'm your mother."

"Well, I want to share something with you that happened about three hours ago," I went on. "Remember when I was a little kid and found your tampons under the sink . . . "

Somehow I wish the conversation had been different. Even though she offered all kinds of encouragement, I knew she was feeling the distance between us. We were sharing only words.

Rachel came over after supper.

"I just want to check up on you." She smiled. "Are you crampy?"

"I'm fine," I told her.

"Are you self-conscious that you're wearing something?"

"I always thought I would be. But it's like the bra, I have to remind myself that it's really happened."

"I have a confession," she said. "You want to hear something silly?"

I nodded. "Always."

"When my mom bought me my first box of pads, even before I'd started, I used to wear them around just to get used to them. Isn't that stupid?"

"Not at all," I told her.

My period is really light today. I know this is normal for the first time and Rachel says that the same thing happened to her. "It took me four or five before they lasted a week. And I skipped one once."

My period. What a strange thing to write when I think how I felt three months ago.

Mr. Wardcourt came through in fine form with lecture number three. It was on good posture.

"Good posture is one of the most important things you can achieve," the assistant principal declared. "Standing up straight and tall shows a proud, healthy body supported by a healthy mind."

Chuck bent over and acted like Igor in those old monster movies.

"When I see the citizens of tomorrow slouching and bent over, I worry about the future of our fine country," Mr. Wardcourt went on. "Bent backs mean bent thoughts. Bent thoughts mean bent deeds."

Mr. Manning was listening to this with his elbow propped on the desk and his chin resting on his right hand. He peered at the assistant principal under his eyebrows. "Whoa," he broke in. "Where in heaven's name do you get such ridiculous ideas from anyway?"

Mr. Wardcourt's forehead went red and he pinched his shoulder blades together. He stared into Mr. Manning's face with an expression that would have scared the spit out of me.

"I beg your pardon?" His voice oozed anger.

Mr. Manning waved his left hand in the air. "If I wrote down what you're saying in a story, an editor would tell me my dialogue wasn't realistic."

"What do you mean?" Mr. Wardcourt demanded.

Exactly what I wanted to know.

"I mean, you're talking gobbledygook," Mr. Manning explained.

I could almost see the steam rising from the assistant principal's scalp. "We'll discuss this later, Mr. Manning. In my office. At recess."

"No, we won't. I have to write a story then." Mr. Manning smiled.

Mr. Wardcourt took a deep breath that made his nostrils flare out. "It is plain to see who stands with a bent back in this classroom."

"It's more comfortable." Mr. Manning continued to smile.

I've long since realized that Mr. Manning isn't a normal teacher, but I *do* know, normal or not, teachers aren't allowed to act like that.

Everyone thinks this is going to mean trouble.

Friday, November 28

Derek said hello to me in choir today. It's the first time we've spoken since we had the "ballet" talk. It's the first time he's really noticed me since then. He didn't seem mad. In fact, he was really friendly. I asked him how his hockey team was doing. He just nodded his head and said "Okay." as if he didn't want to talk about it.

Mr. Gowing has us doing "Jingle Bell Rock" and "I Wish Every Day Could Be Like Christmas" for the Christmas concert this year.

Mr. Gowing is a good music teacher but he's strange in his own way. He walks around muttering to himself. And he wears a heavy gold bracelet which rattles while he is directing us.

During homeroom our class voted to put on a special presentation for the Christmas concert. We're going to do our own version of Ebenezer Scrooge.

Jeeny came to school with makeup on today. She says that her mom is easing up on her. I saw Hank waiting for her at 3:30 and they headed for the Mall.

"Looks like the old Jeeny is back," Rachel said.

I wonder if Jeeny would like to talk again.

Shawn got excited in library today because he found a book which told about something called "spontaneous human combustion."

"Hey, listen to this," he called us around. "It says here there have been cases where people burst into flames for no reason. And they get completely burnt up. Some of the cases have been studied by scientists. Can you imagine anything so awesome?"

"I don't believe it," Marlene said.

"Maybe it'll happen to you," Shawn said.

"I've heard of it," Rachel told everyone.

"Just think what would happen if Mr. Manning caught fire," Shawn said. "Wouldn't that be an awesome Social class?"

"Sometimes you're really sick, Shawn," I pointed out.

Shawn smiled at me. "Suppose you were sitting in class writing in your journal and you burst into flames. Wouldn't that be great?"

"'Course, it could happen to you, Shawn," Rachel reasoned. "That would be even better."

"We could roast marshmallows," Chuck added.

"I'm going to bring my camera to school on Monday," Shawn declared. "If anybody goes up in smoke, I'll be ready to record it."

Monday, December 1

Everybody is stunned.

We can't believe it.

Mr. Manning is being fired!

He told us this *awful* news in Social this morning.

"As some of you have noticed, I'm having a few difficulties with the powers that be. Because of this, I'll be leaving Pine Grove at Christmas. When you return in the new year, you'll have a new teacher for English and Social."

Immediately, there was a chorus of protest.

"Thanks," Mr. Manning said, "but the decision has already been made."

"Are you being fired?" Kevin asked.

Mr. Manning smiled. "Let's just say I've been convinced that this is the best way to solve certain difficulties."

"Don't you like us?" Rachel asked.

"That has nothing to do with it," Mr. Manning explained. "I've enjoyed this class more than any other I've taught. That's the truth. But if I stay, well . . . let's just say, things wouldn't get any better."

As I said, nobody can believe it.

"Do you think he's being fired because he's so weird?" Rachel asked.

"The fact that he's weird is what makes him a great teacher," I pointed out. "Even Marlene agrees with that now. Mr. Gowing is weird and he's a good music teacher. It should have nothing to do with keeping Mr. Manning's job."

Everybody is mad at Mr. Wardcourt. Rachel, Jeeny and I went to his office at lunch to ask if there was anything we could do to make Mr. Manning stay.

"Nothing at all," he said sternly. "In fact, I am very pleased with what has happened. And you should be as well."

"We have to do something about this,"

Rachel told a group of kids after we'd returned from Mr. Wardcourt's office. "We can't let them do this to one of the best teachers in the world."

"The *very* best," I added.

"What can we do?" Chuck wanted to know. "Manning said he had to go."

"What about getting our parents to help?" Kevin suggested.

"Maybe," Rachel agreed. "But we've got to make Old Lady Haines and Mr. Panek know how we feel. We have to do something that's going to bring attention to this injustice," she preached. "Something ultra-radical."

"I don't like this," Marlene said.

"We could burn down the school," Shawn suggested.

"What do you have in mind?" Kevin asked.

"I don't know yet," Rachel said. "Let me think about it."

Everybody is so depressed.

Tuesday, December 2

We're all set for tomorrow. I'm scared about what we're going to do, but it seems like the best thing. It may be the only way to show them that they can't fire Mr. Manning.

Rachel called me last night to tell me her plan. At first I wasn't sure, but now it seems perfect.

"I want you to call these kids tonight." Rachel listed five people in our class. "Tell them to meet us outside first thing in the morning . . ."

We had a big meeting outside before first bell.

"Okay, everyone," Rachel said, "I think I've got a plan. The way I see it, there's nothing to stop us as a class from going downtown to Mr. Panek's office and having a little protest, is there?"

"What do you mean?" Jeeny asked.

"Well," Rachel explained, "instead of coming to school tomorrow, we all get the bus to the board office. We'll go sit in front of Panek's door until they rehire Mr. Manning."

"All right!" some of the kids cheered.

"We can order pizzas," Chuck pointed out.

Rachel stared at him for a few moments before returning her attention to the rest of us. "We can call the TV people," she said. "We'll make the whole city know how unfairly they're treating Mr. Manning."

There was another big cheer.

And, so far, it seems that everyone in the class is going to go, even Marlene.

She was balking until Rachel asked her to imagine what life would be like without Mr. Manning.

"We'd learn more," Marlene reasoned.

"Dumb stuff like fur trade routes," Chuck countered. "Manning is cool. He knows what we're all about."

"Chuck's right," I told Marlene. "It could get a lot worse. Besides, they can't fire him just because he's different from other teachers. That isn't fair."

"I guess not," she mumbled.

"We need you, Marlene," I said. "We need everyone."

"All right," she nodded. "I'll tell my parents."

"Don't do that." Rachel said. "You're going to have to make up your own mind on this, Marlene." Then she spoke to everybody. "Nobody can tell their parents anything. If one parent learns about it, it could blow the whole thing."

We're sworn to secrecy.

Mr. Manning is sitting at his desk writing a story. Little does he dream that he has a seventh grade army ready to do battle for him.

Thursday, December 4

There's a funny atmosphere at school today. On the one hand, everyone is buzzing over what happened at the board offices yesterday. But, at the same time, it's amazing how fast things have returned to normal. We had our regular classes today as if *nothing* had happened.

Mr. Manning wasn't here today. Mrs. Byrd was our sub. Mr. Wardcourt told us Mr. Manning would be back tomorrow, that he had to meet with Mr. Panek and some parents downtown to sort some things out.

I was really scared when I caught the bus with half my class on Wednesday morning. I'd never even skipped out before, let alone taken part in a demonstration. The rest of the class was waiting for us when we arrived at the Center for Education. Everybody showed up — even Marlene.

"I'm still not sure about this," Marlene frowned. "Perhaps it wasn't such a good idea for me to come."

"We're all proud of you," Rachel said.

"Way to go, Marlene." Chuck slapped her shoulder.

"Ow," she complained.

I found myself walking beside Rachel as we led twenty-three seventh graders from Pine Grove School into the big, blue building.

We marched up to the reception desk. A balding, paunchy security guard eyed us suspiciously. "What do you want?" he asked.

"Mr. Panek's office, please," Rachel said.

"Third floor," he told us. "But I hardly think he's expecting this many . . . "

We walked to the elevators.

Half the class went up and then the rest of us. They have these neat glass elevators which overlook a greenhouse-like courtyard. At this point we lost Chuck. He decided to keep riding them.

Mr. Panek's secretary didn't know what to do as we all tried to crowd through the door into his office. She ended up muttering to herself the way Mr. Gowing does.

By this time other people had come out of their offices to check out what "all the kids" were doing.

Finally, Mr. Panek appeared with a stunned look on his face. "What is going on?" he asked.

The bell rang. I'll continue tomorrow.

I couldn't wait. It's just after supper, about seven o'clock. I took my journal home because I wanted to write everything down while it's still clear in my head.

Besides, I'm grounded for a week with no TV. That's my punishment for taking part in the protest. So writing will give me something to do.

Ralph just knocked on my door and poked his head into my room. "How's my little terrorist sister doing?" he asked.

Anyway, back to yesterday. Mr. Panek didn't know what to do with us. And then the TV people came. Rachel had called them before she left home. And soon everything was happening in front of TV cameras.

"I want you all to return to your school," Mr. Panek ordered.

Nobody moved, except Marlene.

"Stay where you are, Marlene!" Rachel called.

"If you do not return to school immediately,

you may be suspended," Mr. Panek threatened.

Again, only Marlene moved. I grabbed her coat to stop her.

"Solidarity forever!" Shawn yelled.

And there we were, our class, disobeying the superintendent of all the schools in the city, in front of TV cameras.

"Aren't you going to ask why we're here?" Rachel asked the superintendent.

Before Mr. Panek could answer, Rachel turned to a reporter and started to speak at a TV camera. She talked about Mr. Manning and how he was being fired for no good reason and how he was the best teacher in the whole city. A little weird maybe, but still the best. The rest of the class punctuated her speech with applause and cheers.

As soon as Rachel was finished, a reporter pushed a microphone under my chin.

"Why are you here?" she asked.

"To save my teacher's job," I said proudly. "He's a super teacher, even if he does think fur trade routes are dumb. He doesn't deserve to be fired just because nobody wants to buy his stories."

Mr. Panek threatened us with a suspension again.

And once more we had to stop Marlene.

Shawn said that if we lit a match under the smoke detectors, we could get the fire department down and cause a real mess.

Kevin made him settle down.

It was all so exciting. And for a few minutes I thought we were going to get Mr. Manning's job back. I mean, how could they refuse? They couldn't move us until we got what we wanted.

Dream on, Shannon.

It ended when they phoned our parents. I've never seen so many surprised people. Mothers and fathers called out of work or from home to get their kids from the Center for Education when they were supposed to be in school.

One by one our ranks were thinned by parents toting our classmates home.

Marlene's dad looked like he was going to have a heart attack.

There were only Jeeny, Shawn, Rachel and me left when Mr. Manning appeared.

"You guys." He smiled, "What am I going to do with you? When I saw the empty classroom I thought maybe it was Saturday."

"We don't want you to leave," I told him.

"I'm . . . I don't know what to say to you . . . " Mr. Manning mumbled. "This is something else."

The TV cameras were filming the whole thing.

"We'll save your job," Shawn declared.

Mr. Manning nodded. "Did you ever think to ask me if I wanted the job?"

"Huh?" I asked. "What do you mean?"

"Let's go downstairs and wait for your

folks," he suggested. "We'll talk about it at school."

As we were leaving, my father and Rachel's mom arrived. We were explaining what had happened as we got on the elevator.

"Hey, guys," Chuck Hillman said.

"You been here all this time?" Jeeny asked.

He nodded. "You want to go up to the roof?"

"Come on, Chuck," Mr. Manning said. "Let's go home."

What a time! To think that a bunch of kids could cause so much excitement. Jeeny Carter said she saw it on the national news at eleven o'clock.

I hope Mr. Manning comes back tomorrow.

Friday, December 5

It turns out that we were wasting our time at the Center for Ed. Mr. Manning came back today and explained what he meant.

He doesn't want to be a teacher anymore!

"I have to tell you how much what you did means to me," he told us. "It was incredible. Nobody has done anything like that for me before. Thank you very, very much."

Everybody was silent.

"But," he went on, "I don't want to keep my job. I guess I should have told you everything on Monday. I wasn't fired. I don't fit at Pine Grove School and my leaving was a mutual decision."

"What's that mean?" Chuck asked.

"It means Mr. Panek and I both agreed that my leaving was the best thing for everyone, including you. You guys deserve much better."

There was a howl of protest.

"I mean it," he went on. "I've been slacking off in class. I've been more interested in my stories than in teaching you what I'm supposed to."

"You're a great teacher," Rachel said.

He smiled at us. "Bottom line, the fact is, I'm not happy being a teacher anymore. I need some time to try something else. Do you understand?"

Again, there was silence.

"Now let's catch up on that fur trade stuff that I was supposed to teach you a month ago."

Time's up.

After supper — at home.

I stayed behind to talk to Mr. Manning after school. Rachel stayed with me.

"I understand you girls were the leaders of Wednesday's excitement," he said.

"Not really," I told him. "It was a class thing."

He nodded. "Well, thanks again."

"Mr. Manning," I said, "before you, I thought teachers were . . . well, they weren't real people."

He laughed.

"But you showed me how wrong that is.

You're just a person." I thought for a moment, then I added, "I mean that in a nice way."

Mr. Manning smiled at me. "I know what you mean."

I stared at him.

"Is there something bothering you, Shannon?" he asked.

"Everything is changing," I said. "Who would have thought you'd leave? Who'd have thought the seventh grade would be such . . . " I stopped. "I don't know what I want to say. Just, who would have thought?"

Classic
School
Exercise
Book

Name: <u>Shannon</u>

School: <u>University of Pine Grove</u>

Teacher: ~~Mr. M~~ <u>Mrs. B.</u>

Subject: <u>Journal Number 4</u>

The vampire stared into my eyes.

"You're mine now, Shannon MacKenzie,"
the vampire hissed. "You'll have to walk with
the undead forever."

"It's better than living here." I smiled into
his red eyes.

"You mean you want to be a vampire?"

"You get to wear nice clothes," I pointed out.

"It's the pits working at night," he ex-
plained.

"You should try being grounded," I grum-
bled.

And still another Keytab.

Is it ever boring being grounded. I can take
being in the house all day — but the no TV is
killing me.

I brought Dad a lunch of macaroni and
cheese and a beer into the TV room.

"Is this a sneaky way to watch TV?" he
asked.

"Believe it or not, I'm not into Australian
Rules Football," I told him.

"It's a great sport."

"That would be worse than no TV."

He glanced at the tray. "I'll take the food,
but put the Bud back in the fridge. I'm not here
for the day. Irene and I are going to the home
show."

"You guys are getting along great."

He nodded. "She's something else. What are you going to do today?"

"Nothing. What else can I do? I'm stuck here all day. Maybe I'll write in my journal later."

"You know, Shannon, despite the fact that I grounded you, I'm proud of you. I'm proud you did something you believed in."

"You didn't seem proud on Wednesday."

"I was angry because you hadn't told me." Dad said. "I was angry because you went downtown without telling me."

"And what if I had told you?"

"I wouldn't have let you go."

We both started laughing. He held out his arms and we hugged. We don't do that very often.

"I love you, Shannon," he said.

After supper.

The day drags on. Rachel, who isn't grounded, phoned and told me she saw Derek in the Mall. She said he was asking about me.

Jeeny Carter dropped by, but I couldn't let her in because of the grounding. She's back to her old (new?) self — straight, messy hair with lots of makeup. She showed me a necklace with a ring on it. It looked expensive.

"It means Hank and I are going steady," she told me.

I didn't know whether to congratulate her or offer my sympathy.

The necklace is probably stolen.

I'm going to try and go to sleep. What else is there to do?

Sunday, December 7

The only problem with going to bed early Saturday night is Sunday morning. What do you do at six o'clock Sunday morning?

I spent the morning reading back through my Keytabs. All the stuff that has happened!

And only two more weeks until Christmas break. Only two more weeks of Mr. Manning.

I guess I'm going to have to get used to the fact that he won't be around anymore. I guess you can get used to anything. Look at how my feelings about THE BIG P have changed.

Dad asked me what I wanted for Christmas. I told him clothes.

Not only puberty, but the first sign of old age. Clothes for Christmas! But that's what I *really* want. There is no hope. I'm over the line.

Monday, December 8

Mom called on Sunday night and we talked for over an hour.

"Let's make Sunday our night," she suggested. "Would it be all right if I called every Sunday evening? We could make it our time. What do you think, honey?"

"I think that's a great idea, Mom," I agreed.

"I'd like to look forward to that."

"So would I," she said. "I want to know everything that's happening in your life."

So I told her about Mr. Manning and the scene at the board offices.

"You're certainly growing up in a hurry, aren't you?" was her response.

And I told her about Derek and the other kids in my class. About Rachel, Jeeny, Shawn, Kevin. Even Chuck.

Speaking of Chuck: He just started his second journal book today. He's stopped writing swear words. Now he's writing words that sound gross.

"You see," he told me, "I take a word that sounds gross just because of the way it sounds."

"Huh?" I said. "What do you mean?"

"Well, you take the word 'puke' — that sounds gross, right?"

"I'm not sure I want to hear any more."

"What I do is take the word 'puke' and use it in a sentence that makes it even grosser. Want to hear one?"

"No way." I shook my head. "Keep it to yourself."

He ignored me. "How about, 'I had a puke sandwich for lunch'?"

"Gross me out! I said I didn't want to hear it."

"Or," he went on, "how about, 'Excuse me, Ms MacKenzie, can I borrow a cup of puke?'"

I felt my stomach heave. "Shut up, Chuck!"

"Upchuck?" he grinned. "Thanks for the word."

"Something wrong back there?" Mr. Manning asked.

"We were just talking about our journals," Chuck said.

"Keep it down," Mr. Manning told us.

"Keep it down," Chuck whispered. "Upchuck. Keep it down. Get it?"

Gross! Disgusting! How can he live with those thoughts going around in his head?

We have choir practice every lunch from now on. The Christmas concert is next Tuesday night.

Tuesday, December 9

We planned our Christmas concert skit today. Mr. Manning found an old play of Scrooge in the library. We should be able to cut it down to about five minutes.

Rachel suggested that the kids who weren't on the stage could sing a short carol as each ghost appeared. Everyone thought that was a great idea.

"It would be neat if Jacob Marley was on fire when he was talking to Scrooge," Shawn suggested.

"I vote Shawn play the part of Marley," Rachel said.

Shawn got selected for the part, although

Mr. Manning convinced him that being wrapped in chains would be more effective than renting an asbestos suit.

Jeeny is going to play Scrooge. Chuck thought that was stupid. "Everybody knows that Scrooge is a guy. And everybody knows Jeeny is a girl."

"You noticed?" Jeeny snarled. "I bet Hank Johnston thinks I can be a good Scrooge. Do you want me tell him you don't, Chuck?"

Chuck changed his mind.

Chuck is the Ghost of Christmas Past. I'm the Ghost of Christmas Present, and Marlene is Christmas Future. Kevin is Bob Cratchit, Rachel will lead the carol singers, and Mr. Manning is Tiny Tim.

We all thought that it would be funny for Mr. Manning to be Tiny Tim because he's so tall and his moustache. At first he didn't want to do it, but we talked him into it.

Derek asked me to his hockey game tomorrow night. And I'm going.

He came up to me in choir and said, "Hi, Shannon. How's it going?"

"Not bad," I told him.

"You've been looking really nice," he went on. "I like the way you've been doing your hair."

I haven't been doing anything with my hair, except growing it. But it was a nice thing to say.

"I was wondering if you'd like to come to my

hockey game at Millwoods Rec Center tomorrow. We're playing for first place."

"Well, I . . ."

"If you haven't got anything else to do, that is," he said. "Like ballet."

I laughed. "No ballet," I told him. "I'm just thinking if I'm still grounded. But that's finished tonight. What time?"

"Seven-thirty," he smiled. "It's in Millwoods A."

Why not?

Chuck just asked me if I wanted to hear the great sentences he's made with the word "snot."

Thanks, but no thanks.

Thursday, December 11

We didn't do U.S.S.W. yesterday because we rehearsed Scrooge. What a wipe-out. Shawn brought these chains to do Marley. He locked himself up and then lost the key. Mr. Owens, the janitor, had to saw the lock open.

I went to watch Derek last night. What a great game. His team lost 3-2. But only because the referee was on the other team's side.

It took me about five minutes to notice how unfair the ref was. So I started screaming all sorts of things at him. Stuff about his eyesight and needing glasses. Once someone tripped Derek and didn't get a penalty.

"Get in the game, ref!" I hollered.

I waited outside the dressing room to say hello, and when Derek saw me his face lit up.

"I'm glad you waited for me," he said.

"The ref is as blind as a peeled potato."

"Huh?"

"A peeled potato," I explained. "You know, no eyes."

Derek laughed, but I know he didn't understand my simile.

Then he introduced me to his dad. Talk about big. His dad is like a Sasquatch. Huge — and his face is covered with a thick red beard.

Mr. Anderson looked me up and down and smiled. "A pretty lady. Just like Derek has been telling me for the last two months."

Derek's face went all red.

"We're going to McDonald's," Mr. Anderson said. "You want to grab a burger with us?"

So I ended up eating french fries with Derek and his dad and talking about hockey.

"Hockey sure is different when you know someone in the game," I said.

"You get right into it," Derek's dad agreed.

Then I told Mr. Anderson my opinion of the referee.

"Was that *you* shouting? You sure have a powerful voice."

I felt embarrassed.

"But it's good to have spirit," Derek's dad went on. "What are you into, Shannon? You play sports? Got any hobbies?"

"Shannon used to take ballet," Derek said.

His dad nodded to himself as Derek and I laughed.

Friday, December 12

I just spent a few minutes looking around the class. You now, I'm glad I'm here. I'm glad I'm in the seventh grade with this bunch of people. Chuck included.

Everyone feels so close to Mr. Manning now. I've never felt like this with a teacher before. It's like we're all sharing something special.

We rehearsed Scrooge again and ended up laughing so loud Mr. Manning let us go early.

Chuck was wearing his Christmas Past costume, which is a big robe-dress his mother made for him. When Scrooge was supposed to touch the robe to go back into the past, Jeeny tripped and ripped the costume. Everybody saw Chuck's underwear. It had pictures of teddy bears on it.

Chuck turned red and Rachel laughed so hard that Mr. Manning had to help her into the hall to catch her breath.

I babysat little Marty while Dad and Irene went out for dinner. He's such an obnoxious brat. He called me a dumpy fumpy and then proceeded to laugh himself into a fit. Every time he ran through the living room he screamed, "Hi, dumpy fumpy."

We won't have any classes next Monday afternoon. We're being the audience for the elementary Christmas concert. Theirs is on Monday night. On Tuesday we'll rehearse ours for the little kids.

Little kids. Six months ago I was a little kid.

Tuesday, December 16

After school.

There was no U.S.S.W. yesterday because of the elementary concert practice. They were okay, lots of cute performances by the kindergarten and first graders.

"Doesn't this stuff make you want to puke?" was Jeeny's opinion.

I thought it wasn't that bad.

There was no U.S.S.W. today because of our practice. The junior high Christmas concert begins in exactly four hours.

The choir is definitely ready. We sounded terrific at rehearsal this afternoon. Mr. Gowing asked the girls to wear dark skirts, or slacks and white blouses. Same for the boys. No skirts, of course. We should look as great as we sound.

But our Scrooge skit — what a mess! I've only got three lines: "Come with me, Ebenezer," "Behold Tiny Tim," and "Time to go now." But I keep forgetting them. Same with everyone else.

On the stage we kept bumping into each

other. Mr Wardcourt spent most of the time shaking his head.

"We'll be the laughing stock of the concert," Marlene worried.

"Float with it, Marlene," Rachel told her.

We had a talk-time session before U.S.S.W. Mr. Manning told us about Christmas when he was a kid.

"We didn't have any lights for the Christmas tree. All we had were these special Christmas candles. We only lit them for a few minutes on Christmas Eve."

He chuckled to himself. "It was so stupid. Think about lighting candles on a dry tree in your house. My father lit them while my mother stood behind him with a bucket of water."

Shawn thinks that's the most moving story he's ever heard. "Really hits home what Christmas is all about," he said.

Wednesday, December 17

We were the hit of the concert. Not the choir, although we sang just great. And looked it too. Mr. Gowing had this white shirt with ruffles. He looked really handsome. But our Scrooge thing carried the night.

Jeeny sprayed white stuff on her hair so she'd look old, but she kept on her black makeup. She looked like a rock star. Her dad's dressing gown kept coming undone and everybody got to see Scrooge in jeans and a heavy metal T-shirt.

Hank Johnston, who had come to see Jeeny, kept hooting about "the foxy-looking Scrooge."

Chuck's robe stayed on, but he tripped in it once and pulled Jeeny on top of him.

I got completely confused. Maybe I was nervous being in front of all the parents. When I pointed to Mr. Manning, I said, "Behold Tom Thumb." It must have been a good minute until the laughter died down enough for us to carry on.

Marlene (Christmas Future) knew all her lines, but she started over-acting. She'd walk to the front of the stage to say every line to the audience. It was so obvious. I could tell Jeeny was getting upset.

The biggest laugh came when Jeeny (Scrooge) presented the turkey to Kevin (Mr. Cratchit) and Mr. Manning (Tiny Tim).

"What's that, Mr. Scrooge?" Mr. Manning said.

"It used to be the Ghost of Christmas Future," Jeeny snarled.

That broke everybody up. They thought it was part of the play.

All in all, the best concert ever.

My dad said it was refreshing to see something original. "These things usually make me nod off."

Then he said, "It's too bad your mom

couldn't have seen you. I'm sure she'd be proud of you."

I'll tell her during our time on Sunday.

Thursday, December 18

We hardly did any work today. Tomorrow we're going to have a party in our double English. To celebrate the Christmas holidays and to say goodbye to Mr. Manning. We planned who would bring what.

Kevin is going to bring his CD player and we're bringing our favorite CDs. Mr. Manning is going to let us have a dance in the room and we can invite the other seventh grade class. It's been arranged with Mr. Wardcourt.

Rachel has been collecting money from everybody all week. The class wants to buy Mr. Manning an expensive pen to write his stories with.

Mr. Manning read us his kids' story today. I don't think he has much future writing for young people either.

It was about a seventh grade girl who could make time stop whenever she snapped her fingers.

Whenever this girl got upset, she'd snap and the whole world would stop. Every time she had a problem, she'd just snap it away until she felt ready to face it again.

It didn't sound so bad at first, but the girl in the story used her snap so often that she died of old age before her class finished the Christmas concert.

Seriously, now!

But believe it or not, I think I understand this one. It has something to do with the fact that you can't run away and hide from stuff.

Chuck Hillman told me he could think of some wonderful things to do if he could stop the world. I told him keep them to himself.

Less than a month to my birthday.

Saturday, December 20

Marlene asked Mr. Manning if there was going to be any homework over Christmas. He just laughed.

Then he said, "You know, it might not be a bad idea to take your journals home. Something could happen that you might want to write about."

All kinds of stuff happens I want to write about. I've become a journal junkie.

The dance was kind of happy and sad at the same time. Most of the class danced. Even Chuck. You should have seen Chuck trying to boogie after Rachel dared Jeeny to ask him.

Derek danced with a couple of the other girls, but mostly me. He even danced the slow ones with me when a lot of the kids wouldn't dance.

Rachel asked Mr. Manning to dance with

her — a fast one. And he did. He didn't move so bad for an old guy. We all clapped when it was over.

Shawn asked Marlene to dance one time and she said she only knew how to waltz. I bet she was lying. Nobody knows how to do that stuff anymore.

Chuck ate two big boxes of potato chips and got sick.

"Think of all the creative sentences for the word 'vomit,' " I told him.

That didn't impress him. But at least it was a little bit of revenge.

Mr. Wardcourt stuck his head in the door a few times, looking more bewildered every time. Once he came in while we were slow dancing. His eyes opened like he'd never seen anyone holding another person before.

Then it was clean-up time. We all crowded around Mr. Manning's desk and Rachel gave him the goodbye card and the pen.

I signed the card: "Keep writing those terrific stories — Thanks, Shannon."

Mr. Manning read the card and looked at the pen and gave us a big smile. I thought he might start crying, but he didn't.

"I'm going to miss you guys an awful lot," he said.

"What are you going to do?" Shawn asked.

"Actually, I'm going someplace warm for a couple of months and I'm going to try to write a YA novel."

"A what?" Chuck asked.

"A book for young adults," Mr. Manning explained. "For people your age."

"About us?" Rachel wondered.

"Probably. Whatever I do, I'm going to remember all the good times we had — and a certain Wednesday in December."

Everybody cheered. Some of us were crying when the bell rang.

And, for the last time, Rachel and I stayed behind to talk to Mr. Manning. He was throwing the stuff from his desk into a box.

"You sure you don't know who's going to be our new teacher?" Rachel asked.

"I'm positive. How many times have I told you that?"

Rachel shrugged. "I figured maybe you were trying to hide it from us. You don't want to tell us Mr. Wardcourt is going to be our new teacher."

Mr. Manning laughed. "Can you see bozo brain trying to teach a class?"

Rachel and I laughed even though it wasn't respectful and was downright rude. But who was going to know?

"Mr. Manning," I said, "may I ask you a personal question?"

"As long as I don't have to answer."

"You told us that you live alone, but were you ever married?" I asked. "Do you have any kids?"

"Shannon!" Rachel made as if she was surprised, although I knew she was dying to find out too.

Mr. Manning smiled. "Yeah, I used to be married. My ex-wife lives in Ontario."

"I'm sorry," I said.

He smiled. "Sorry my ex-wife lives in Ontario? I'm not. We don't really like each other anymore. She thinks I'm weird."

I can understand that.

"Any kids?" I asked.

He nodded. "A son in the seventh grade and a daughter in the fifth grade."

"I bet your son is cute," Rachel said.

"Just like his old man." Mr. Manning nodded.

"Do they live in Ontario too?" I asked.

"They do," he said softly. "A long way away. And if I can guess your next question — I miss them very much."

"Life sometimes isn't fair, is it?" I pointed out.

Mr. Manning gave me a warm smile that made wrinkles round his eyes. "Shannon, things change."

"Tell me about it," I scoffed.

He shook hands with Rachel and me and said he had the feeling we'd meet again.

So that's it for Mr. Manning.

People come into your life, stay for a while and leave.

I tried to remember my first grade teacher. Ms Pratt was her name and I think she had a pretty face, but I can't see it in my mind. I guess I could rummage through some boxes and dig out the old class picture. But the fact is I don't remember her anymore.

Ms Pratt has gone. She's not part of my life anymore. She may still be teaching in Dallas. Maybe she's moved someplace else. It doesn't really matter.

As Mr. Manning said, "Things change."

Sunday, December 21

Ralph brought Donna home last night. She's the one he met at Mr. Submarine. They played Monopoly in the kitchen.

Donna is tall and has blonde hair. She'd be pretty if her nose wasn't so big. She's perfect for my brother, though. All evening they talked about cars.

Rachel and I are going to the Mall to do our Christmas shopping tomorrow. And I'm going to another of Derek's games tomorrow night. He phoned and asked me today.

Dad ate over at Mrs. Fox's tonight. Mom called when he was away and we had another long talk. I told her about the party and Derek, and she told me about folding paper and how they were going to Morton's mother's house for Christmas dinner. I like "our time."

I wonder if Mr. Manning is someplace warm yet?

I finished my Christmas shopping. I got Dad one of those key chains where you whistle and it plays a little song — just in case he loses his keys in the snow. And I got Ralph a pen with a girl on it. When you tip the pen upside down, the girl's dress vanishes and she's wearing a bikini.

Rachel says my taste is in my mouth. She bought her mom chocolates and her dad a pair of gloves. Talk about no taste. Everybody gives that stuff. At least I searched for personal gifts.

We ran into Hank and Jeeny. Hank had a big gold cross in his ear.

"How's it ***** going?" Hank asked us.

"Just ***** great," Rachel told him.

Both Jeeny and I were surprised. Rachel never swears.

"Once won't hurt," she told me later.

Then we met Shawn and Chuck. They were playing "Gotcha" with a water pistol full of water and red food color. They were taking turns chasing each other through the Mall.

"There's this fat security guard after us," Chuck bragged.

Shawn showed us what he'd bought for his folks — a propane torch. "You can weld with this," he told us.

"Your folks big on welding?" I asked.

Shawn shook his head. "Naw, but I figure

it's a hobby they might be interested in taking up."

Then the guys saw the security guard and ran away.

After supper I went to the Rec Center to watch Derek. This time I sat with his dad. Mr. Anderson had to tell me to keep my voice down. Apparently I called the referee a "Hank Johnston" word.

And I didn't even know I'd said it.

Mr. Anderson didn't seem to be upset, though. "I agree with your opinion," he chuckled, "but let's keep it to ourselves."

We went to McDonald's again after the game and Mr. Anderson invited me over for supper on Boxing Day.

What a neat day. Everything went well. Everyone was friendly. I love Christmas.

I just started my period again. Hey, that's pretty close to being right on — almost average. Not bad for only two tries, if I do say so myself.

Christmas

I got exactly what I wanted under the Christmas tree — clothes. I was really surprised because they all fit and they were all in style. I had visions of trucking the boxes back to the store to exchange them. My father is not exactly a great shopper.

"These are terrific, Dad," I told him.

He was beaming like he'd done something wonderful. "I didn't pick them out," he said. "Irene did."

My gifts were the hit of the morning. Just like I thought. Dad's key ring is so neat. You whistle and it plays this song which Dad says is a waltz. Trouble is, it starts playing when you don't whistle too. The tape deck or the TV will set it off. Even talking. It played so often that the battery is worn out already.

Ralph thought his pen was super. "Kind of crud art. I like stuff like this, Shannon."

Mrs. Fox and Marty came by after lunch. I had to pig out again on ham and Christmas pudding.

Mrs. Fox kept on asking me if I wanted to help her in the kitchen. I said no. Rachel says it's sexist to think that girls have to cook. And I agree, even though I'm not sure what "sexist" means.

Turned out that Ralph helped her anyway.

Mom called to wish us all a Merry Christmas. Dad spoke to her for several minutes. Before he said goodbye, he said, "All the best in whatever you do, Susan." It was a nice thought.

I went into the living room just in time to see little Marty wipe out the Christmas tree. The ornaments that used to belong to Grandma ended up in little glass splinters over the carpet.

Dad and Ralph were laughing, but I wanted

to destroy the little creep. You can only have so much Christmas spirit.

Boxing Day

I had a good time at Derek's house. His mom made lasagna, my favorite meal. Derek got a tabletop hockey game for Christmas. We ended up playing that with his dad.

Then Derek and I went down to the family room alone. We watched TV and he held my hand.

"This is real great," Derek said. "I'm glad you came over."

Even though my hand got all sweaty, I didn't want to let go of Derek.

"I'm sorry about before," I told him.

"That's okay."

"I don't know why I gave you a hard time about hockey. I was worried about other stuff at the time."

"I said it's okay. I'm glad you're not worried anymore."

"Maybe I am," I told him, "But I'm having fun too."

I wondered if he was going to try to kiss me. We *were* downstairs, with his folks upstairs. But he didn't.

Thursday, January 1

Happy New Year and all that.

Mr. Anderson asked Dad if I could spend New Year with them. Derek's folks had some friends over. They danced in the basement and had a buffet meal at midnight. Derek and I danced and I could see all the adults smiling at us as if they thought we were cute or something.

It was close to two o'clock when Mr. Anderson drove me home.

Saturday, January 3

Another hockey game last night with Derek. His mom joined me in cheering and screaming. We make a great pair of fans.

After, we went back to Derek's place for hot chocolate. Derek and I got to sit in the family room alone again. We watched the Oilers game on TV. He held my hand, but he didn't try to kiss me.

It's not that I'm *dying* to kiss Derek. It's just that I'm curious. When you kiss your relatives it's no great thing. But when I see girls and guys on TV kissing, then it seems as if there is something else to it. They look like they're enjoying it.

Derek doesn't seem as curious as I am, though. I even dropped a hint, but he didn't catch on.

"Derek," I said, "do you remember when you went to see *The Slime* with Jeeny Carter?"

"Yeah." He nodded. "It was a good movie."

"Well, did you hold Jeeny's hand then?"

He made a pained expression as if he was thinking hard. "No. I was eating a jumbo butter popcorn."

"So you didn't kiss her then?" I asked.

"'Course I didn't," he said. "Why would you think that?"

"I was just wondering. Sometimes if a boy and girl are alone, then . . . "

Just then the Oilers scored and he lost my train of thought.

Sunday, January 4

School tomorrow. I wonder what our new teacher will be like. As long as it isn't Mr. Wardcourt.

Monday, January 5

I suppose things could be worse!

Mrs. Byrd, the substitute, is our new homeroom, English and Social teacher.

Chuck started making his famous belching noise in Social. Mrs. Byrd sent him down to Mr. Wardcourt, and Chuck got three days lunchtime DT.

She's so strict. Not at all like when she was a sub. We even have *homework*!

And Mrs. Byrd says this is the last time we'll write our journals in class. "Writing when nobody is going to mark it is a waste of time. It will be more beneficial to examine how nouns and verbs help us express ourselves."

Everybody moaned at the announcement, but I think most people are happy they don't have to write anymore. I know Chuck is. It must have been hard thinking up creative sentences for words like "mucus" and "barf."

Marlene seemed a little upset. "It's wonderful to be a young woman growing up in these exciting times. And it's delightful to record the exciting events that shape our lives."

But I don't think Marlene is *super* upset that she'll be unable to record the "exciting" events of the next five months. She seems to enjoy underlining nouns and circling verbs.

In fact, probably the only person who is truly upset about the end of U.S.S.W. is me. I'm going to miss it.

But I've decided to write at home for a while. At least until my birthday.

On Saturday night I'm having a birthday party. You're only thirteen once.

Tuesday, January 6

At home.

Some of us are going swimming at the wave pool tonight.

"January is such a dismal month," Rachel said. "Let's do something. Let's all meet at the wave pool tonight and have a little party."

Chuck thinks it's terrific. "When I grow up, I want to be a party animal," he told us.

I asked Derek to come but he has a hockey practice.

Mrs. Byrd assigned us a Social project — due in three weeks. It has to be about fur traders. Everybody is upset because she's making us do work.

At recess Shawn Nelson started to tell me the different types of fires — how some fires got worse if you threw water on them.

"My folks really liked the propane torch I got them for Christmas," he went on. "I wonder why they haven't used it yet?"

Mr. Wardcourt just came into the class. He looked at us and smiled. "It's so satisfying to see the future citizens of our great country in capable hands."

Wednesday, January 7

At home. After supper.

I've just come back from another of Derek's games. We won 4-3. My throat is raw from shouting so much.

This little kid asked me which one of the players was my boyfriend. I pointed to number eight. That's kind of neat — the thought that I have a boyfriend. It makes me feel grown-up. I wasn't embarrassed at all.

During morning break Chuck got caught walking on the chalk ledge by the supervision teacher. Mr. Wardcourt wasn't too impressed. Poor Chuck got another week lunchtime DT.

Shawn told us that he's moving at the end of January. "My folks bought a house in St. Albert."

"We'll miss you, Shawn," Rachel said. And she wasn't making fun!

"Yeah," Shawn agreed. "I'll miss you guys. But I'm kind of anxious to move. My new house has a fireplace."

Mrs. Byrd told everyone we should be working on our public speeches. "They are due in mid-February."

Marlene informed everyone she's already finished. Her topic is "The Role of Toilets in Providing a Healthy Environment."

Did I think that Mr. Wardcourt's words fell on deaf ears?

We talked about adjectives during U.S.S.W. time. How boring!

And the big news — I got a letter from Mr. Manning. It came to my house and was addressed to me personally.

It says:

Dear Shannon:

Hope you had a good Christmas. I'm writing this in my apartment in a city called Tucson. That's in Arizona, near the Mexican border. It's warm here. When I think of Edmonton in January, I start to shiver.

The reason I'm writing to you is to tell you about the book I'm writing. It's a novel for young people. Not a weird story either! It's more of a "serious-funny" book, if that makes any sense. Well, one of the characters in my story is very much like you. Would you mind if I used your name in the book? I promise your character will be one of the "good" guys.

I'm also writing to Rachel Parsons and a couple of the other people in the class.

Anyway, please write back. I'd like to hear how you're doing.

> Regards,
> John Manning

Wow!

Rachel called to tell me she got a letter too. So did Jeeny. Just think, my name may be in a book. Our names in a book.

Thursday, January 8

At home.

Just came back from babysitting Marty Fox. Dad took Irene out for supper. Marty tried all sorts of stuff like hiding in the pot cupboard and crying when I told him it was bedtime.

I don't think he likes me. Good. 'Cause I don't like him!

I told him that if he didn't stop trying to be a jerk, I'd clean his face with a soap pad. That impressed him. He settled down a whole lot.

You've got to know how to treat little kids.

Derek told me he had Oilers tickets for Sunday night and he wanted to take me to the game as a birthday gift.

Terrific!

Kevin Harke asked Rachel to go roller skating with him on Friday night. Rachel is pretending there's nothing to it, but I think she really likes him.

Some people in the class were upset they hadn't received letters from Mr. Manning. Shawn, Chuck and Marlene got notes as well.

Marc said that it didn't bother him not to be asked because Mr. Manning's stories were always weird and this one would be as well.

"How do you know?" I asked.

"Well, just look," Marc explained. "He's picked all the weird people to be in it."

Mrs. Byrd told us that studying the parts of speech would help us to understand the works of great writers. So we spent double English writing sentences and listing all the nouns, verbs, adjectives and adverbs. Talk about a numb-out.

The school is going to start taking the really smart kids out of class a couple of periods a week. They call it Program for the Academically Talented, or PAT. Marlene got selected from our class. Figures! And the other person from our class is Chuck Hillman.

Who would have thought that!?

Rachel says the line between insanity and genius is a thin one.

Friday, January 9

Mr. Gowing told us he was going to enter the choir in a competition. We'll have to practice real hard, but we get to go to Calgary for the contest. For three days. During school time. We'll stay in a hotel.

All of a sudden everybody wants to be in the choir, but Mr. Gowing says only the people who have been there since the beginning will be able to go.

Mrs. Byrd asked me, Jeeny and Rachel to go down to the first grade class after lunch. We were each assigned a "buddy" who has to read to us. We're going to do this once a week until the end of school.

My "buddy" is a girl called Shelagh. What kind of way is that to spell Sheila? Parents nowadays! Half the kids in the first grade class have funny names like Selby, Marcus, Roonan, Bartholomew . . . There's even one girl called January.

I feel so sorry for the kids. Peg the kid with a stupid name just because the parents want to be different.

Anyway, Shelagh is kind of a cute kid. She asked me what Santa brought me for Christmas.

The story she was reading was about rabbits. Shelagh asked me if I had a bunny.

Bunny. What a stupid-sounding word.

I'm glad I'm not in the first grade anymore. Things are so boring! All they ever do is read dippy books, listen to dippy stories and think it's a big thrill to put on their paint shirts.

Shelagh says she has to be in bed at "seven-furty."

Seven-thirty! who goes to bed at seven-thirty?

You sure do a lot of growing in six years.

I wrote a letter to Mr. Manning:

Dear Mr. Manning,

Thanks for your letter. I'm glad you're someplace warm. Rachel and I are thinking of running away from home to go someplace warm. Maybe we'll visit you. Ha! Ha! That's a joke!

You ask if you can use my name in your new book? The answer is sure. As long as you pay me $10,000. That's a joke too!

I'm fine. My dad and my brother are okay. They both have serious girlfriends. You found anybody yet? I have. He's Derek Anderson, from the other seventh grade class. You used to teach him English.

Shawn is moving to St. Albert. I'm happy for him because his new house has a fireplace and that seems important in his life.

You know I'm not really the same person you knew even a month ago. And I'm a lot different from the Shannon MacKenzie who started writing in her journal four months ago. Back in September it seemed like everything was changing for the worse. I hated the thought of growing up.

But I've been listening to this first-grader read. And now I'm glad things have changed. I'm glad I'm thirteen years old and growing up.

Things change all the time, don't they? Sometimes the changes are good, sometimes bad. Sometimes awful. And sometimes great! But they do change. So much has changed for me. And things are still changing. But that's life, right? I think you said something like that once.

I hate our new teacher, Mrs. Byrd. She's cancelled U.S.S.W. for verbs and nouns.

You know, when I remember that day at the Center for Education, I start smiling. Remember Chuck riding the elevator?

I hope you'll send me a copy of your book if, no . . . when it gets published.

See you someday.

Your friend,
Shannon Elaine MacKenzie

I'm officially thirteen. So, this is what it's like to be a teenager. Another three hundred and sixty-five days and I'll be fourteen and in eighth grade. Changes.

My dad gave me a "real" pearl necklace for my birthday. He told me that Grandma had given his sister, my Aunt Elsie, a pearl necklace when she turned thirteen.

"It was kind of a special gift to show that she was growing up," he told me. "I realize you're growing up too. Shannon, it just means I love you very much."

Ralph bought me a silver charm bracelet with my first charm on it. It's a little heart.

"Kind of shows what you got lots of," Ralph said. "At least to me."

I cried because I was so happy.

In a few minutes Derek is picking me up to take me to the Oilers game. Last night, at my party, he told me thirteen was such an important age to reach.

"Why?" I asked.

"Because you're allowed to body check in your hockey games."

Guess what else Derek did last night?

He kissed me!

We were dancing to a slow song and holding each other real close. When the song was over he kissed me on the lips.

It wasn't really a kiss, more like a peck. And

it wasn't all that great. He had stuff on his lips from the salt and vinegar potato chips. But at least I can tell Jeeny Carter I know what she's talking about now.

Some of it, anyway.

I invited Chuck to my party because when he found out I was having one, he begged me to let him come. He even offered to give me his journals.

How touching.

I told him he could come as long as I didn't have to take his books of swear words and gross sentences.

Well, Chuck didn't come alone. He brought Marlene!

They were the hit of the party. You should have seen them dance. Marlene told me, "I'm having fun, Shannon. Even though this is a lowbrow activity, I'm definitely having a fine time."

Lowbrow?

Shawn showed up for a little while. He went around trying to practice his public speech on everybody. The topic he chose was 'Forest Fire — A Friend of Trees.'

I'm going to miss Shawn.

Jeeny couldn't make the party. She and Hank had "somewhere else to go." Probably to an arcade to swear at video games. I missed her being there. I think I could have even put up with Hank Johnston.

Rachel and Kevin must have had a good

time roller skating on Friday night. They were very huggy.

"Why fight it?" Rachel said.

Yeah, I guess the real trick is learning what you *can* fight and what you *can't*.

This is going to be the last time I'm going to write in my journal. At least for a while. I've got lots of stuff to do, what with babysitting, Derek, choir and homework. And since we can't do it every day at school, I think I'll take a break.

It's been fun, though. No, not really fun, it's been useful. Maybe in a couple of years I'll pull it out and read the Keytabs again.

See the changes I've been through since today.

The vampire stared into my eyes.

"You're mine now, Shannon MacKenzie," *the vampire hissed. "You'll have to walk with the undead forever."*

"Go away." I smiled into his red eyes.

"You mean you're not afraid of me?"

"After puberty, you're nothing," I pointed *out.*

MARTYN GODFREY is the author of more than two dozen books for young people, including the JAWS Mob series, the Ms Teeny-Wonderful series, and *I Spent My Summer Vacation Kidnapped into Space*. His novel *Mystery in the Frozen Lands* won the Geoffrey Bilson Award for Historical Fiction for Young People.

Martyn was once a junior high teacher like Mr. Manning, but now he writes full-time. He lives in Alberta, and spends most of his non-writing time travelling around the country and talking to kids about books.